The FUN FACTOR

www.matwaugh.co.uk

Produced by Big Red Button Books, a division of
Say So Media Ltd.

Cover design and illustration: Nawrotzky.com

ISBN: 978-1-9999147-0-7

Published: December 2017

Mat Waugh

For Kate

Chapter 1
HEY SUCKERS!

"COME ON DAD, pull harder!"

"That's easy for you to say, sitting up there in your comfy seats," replied Dad. He yanked again at the packing tape and nearly fell over backwards. "It's no good. Thora, hand me those scissors, will you?"

It was about six o'clock and for once we were all in the same room. I passed Dad the scissors from the table and read out loud from the side of the box.

```
ROAM 3 WATCH'N'WINCH VACUUM SOLUTION
     The world's only stair-climbing
            vacuum cleaner.
Now with eye-in-the-sky drone assistance!
```

"That's absurd," said Melissa, without looking up. She was sitting at the cluttered dining table in her smart navy work suit, thumbing through the pages of *Social Policy* magazine (whatever that means).

Some people in my year have boyfriends. I've never had a boyfriend. I'm not even sure I want one. But if I did, I would at least *pretend* to be interested in what they were doing, at least at the start. Melissa obviously didn't agree.

We must have looked a funny bunch. Shannon hadn't changed out of her school uniform, of course, but I was already in my nightie, Reggie in his favourite dinosaur onesie. As for Dad, it wasn't long before he'd be heading out for his nightshift. But for now his skinny white legs stuck out from his pyjama shorts like a couple of hairy drinking straws, twitching as he tried to cut the plastic tape with our rubbish kitchen scissors.

"Why has it got a witch?" asked Reggie. He was sitting next to me on the sofa, playing a racing game on his handheld console. Every time he turned a right hand corner he leaned into me, and I could feel his body twitching as he jabbed his thumbs at the buttons.

"What are you talking about?" I said.

He groaned as his car spun onto the grass, and he looked up at me. "Watch and witch, I heard you say it."

"*Winch*, dumbo, not witch," said Shannon, without taking her eyes off the telly. She didn't take her eyes off the TV much in those days, to be honest. But she glanced over at Dad. "That box is clearly an intelligence test," she said, swinging her legs over the end of sofa, "and I'm not sure you're going to pass."

"Easy, tiger," Dad warned her.

When you're twelve years old like me, you're not allowed to be rude. But Shannon was 17. At that age grown-ups shrug or say *Pfft! Teenagers!* like it's funny, and then they get on with whatever they were doing.

"The winch is what makes it so expensive," said Dad, his voice straining as he tugged. "These babies are about two grand in the shops, you know. I saw a video about them on YouTube."

Shannon gave a long, low whistle. Melissa put down her magazine and looked at Dad in astonishment. "Two thousand pounds? For a vacuum cleaner? Who'd be crazy enough to pay that?"

"People with more money than sense," said Dad, finally flipping open the box and reaching inside. "Still, it didn't cost me a bean so I'm not complaining."

Dad worked at the frozen food factory down the valley. When he was on nights he'd sometimes eat with us before he left, but often he had to go in early to sort stuff out. That's probably why he'd been given the Employee of the Year award. And guess what his prize was? A vacuum cleaner.

Dad pushed the glossy black, domed Roam 3 into the middle of the carpet on hidden wheels.

"It looks like half a Death Star," said Reggie. "Maybe Darth Vader will pop out and chop off Thora's head."

Like every little brother in the world, Reggie is obsessed with *Star Wars*. And like every eight-year-old boy, he likes talking about killing and chopping things.

"Maybe that feature will be on the next model," said Dad, pressing a button on the side of the dome. The Roam 3 started to pulse with a blue glow. "Right, I'll be back in a sec," said Dad, taking the box. "Then we're ready to roam."

Melissa stood up. "Well, I think I can live without the demo. Have you got time for tea before you go out, John?" she asked.

"Bags of time," said Dad. "I don't have to be there 'til eight. Oh, and I brought home some stuff this morning we can have."

"That's good," said Melissa. "It'll be nice to eat together."

"Are you staying here tonight?" I asked.

She sat down next to me on the arm of the sofa. "I haven't decided. Would you mind?"

"Nah," I said.

"Yay!" said Reggie.

"Shannon? How about you?"

Shannon grunted.

"Well, good to get your input," said Melissa briskly as she got up. "Thanks everyone. I'll get the tea on." She headed for the kitchen.

"Let's try the Chicken Wingdings," Dad called after her. "Top drawer of the freezer."

"Oh yes?" Melissa called back.

"They're going down a storm apparently, we're selling them by the truckload."

"I was thinking of something homemade, maybe even healthy," Melissa shouted. "Don't worry, I'll sort something out."

I looked at Dad and pulled a face. He grinned, and headed for the stairs.

"Come on, clip on, you little sod," we heard him say between grunts. "Come on... nearly... there! That's the badger! All sorted." He thumped downstairs again, fished his phone out of his pocket and rested it on top of his potbelly. That's pretty much where his phone used to live – before The Changes, anyway. I wouldn't have been

8

surprised to see a rectangular indent in his tummy, like a human phone holder.

He swiped and tapped for a moment, and the Roam 3 started whistling. Not bleeping, or chirping, or dinging, but proper whistling, like a butcher on a Saturday morning.

"That's weird," said Dad. "I'm not sure what it means, though."

Shannon looked up from the TV. "Maybe it's noticed that the house is filthy and it wants to start work."

"Someone starting work, now there's a novelty," said Dad. "Watch carefully, Shannon, you might learn something."

Shannon huffed. The Roam 3 stopped whistling and shuffled backwards and forwards on the carpet.

"It moved!" shouted Reggie. Dad whooped before leaning over and giving me and Reggie a high five. He held up his hand to Shannon but she looked at him like he was offering her a fish paste sandwich and turned away.

"Suit yourself," said Dad, switching to a deep movie voice. "I have seen the future, and it will clean up our Cheerios."

"You're ridiculous," said Shannon.

"And you're a dead cert for The Least Charming Teenager in the Valley award," said Dad. Shannon gave him a sour look. Dad glanced at the door and lowered his voice. "And while we're talking manners, kids, could you *please* make an effort with Melissa? Just for me?" He lowered his phone and looked at each of us. "Come on guys, it's not easy for her."

"It's not easy for us, either," snapped Shannon. "You meet girls on the internet, bring them home, and suddenly we're supposed to call them mum."

Reggie slid along the sofa towards me and slipped his thumb into his mouth. Melissa had noticed him doing that on her first visit, and told Dad that eight year olds shouldn't suck their thumb. But for once Dad didn't agree. He told her that Reggie had only started doing it when our Mum died, and that you never see a grown-up sucking their thumb, so let's not talk about it. So we didn't.

Dad paused. "That's a bit harsh, Shannon. Think about it. Since... well, since Rosie, I've been living like a monk. Melissa's the first girl – woman – I've met for ages, and I really, *really* like her. Give her a break, if only for me."

"S'pose so," muttered Shannon.

"I like her already," said Reggie.

"Dad," I said.

"Uh-huh?" said Dad, who had returned to his phone. "Dad!"

He looked up. Melissa was standing at the door, smiling.

"Have you got any cheese?" she said.

"Hi!" Dad's face was bright red. "I wasn't talking about you then," he said. "It's... err... another Melissa, lovely girl. She buys frozen fish at head office. I think I might ask her out, you know, go for a few drinks."

"She sounds like just your type," said Melissa, smiling. I liked her better when she smiled. "You should go for it. Now where's the cheese?"

"Third basket from the left, you'll see it – Freezy Cheezy. It's the new extra fine version."

"Your cheese is in the freezer," Melissa said slowly.

"Yes, of course." She shook her head, smiled again, and returned to the kitchen.

"Right, let's get this show on the road," said Dad. "So imagine we've gone out for the day, and asked Roam 3 to clean up."

He leaned over and pressed a button. It sounded just like... well, like a vacuum cleaner. It started to clean in circles, getting bigger every time.

"So it's doing the cleaning," shouted Dad above the noise, "but there's a problem."

Dad picked up some nearby shoes and dropped them in Roam 3's way. Blue lights around the outside started flashing, and Dad's phone made a loud siren noise. Reggie put his hands over his ears.

"So I'm at work, and I don't know what's wrong. I press this *Watch* button on my phone..."

With a soft click, the domed lid scissored open to reveal a shallow mirrored bowl and a drone, its rotors already spinning. It rose steadily into the air until it was about the same height as me and hovered. Even Shannon was watching now.

"Whoah," said Reggie, "that's way cool."

"You bet," said Dad, "and look at this!"

He held his phone up for us to see, and there on the screen was a TV picture of our living room floor, dirty shoes and everything.

"No way!" shouted Shannon.

Reggie and I screamed, and Reggie threw himself to the floor and pulled faces up at the drone.

"And now," shouted Dad above the noise of our shrieks

and the whine of the drone, "I can help it escape! Out of the way Reggie, watch this!"

With a few taps Dad guided the Roam 3 to a clear bit of floor. The drone hovered above, tracking the mothership below, and then on Dad's command it slowly descended into the lid.

"That is wicked," said Shannon. "Stupid, but wicked. Hang on – what happens if it gets trapped under a chair and the drone can't fly up?"

Dad, who was now following the Roam 3 out of the room, paused. "Good point," he said. "I'm not sure they've thought that one through. Still, come and watch this!"

We crowded round the bottom of the stairs.

"Here comes the party trick!"

Click. Whirr. Tick-tick-tick. Out popped the drone again. Only this time it only rose about 30cm into the air, and beneath it hung a thin black cord.

The drone flew slowly up the stairs, extending the cord behind it. We all squeezed up alongside for a better view. "Don't get in the way, it'll chop your head off!" Dad shouted. Now you know where Reggie gets his ideas from.

At the top the drone landed neatly onto the 'Winch Dock', which was basically a miniature heliport that Dad had strapped to the banisters. The cord hanging beneath the drone passed into a slot, and with a couple of clicks, the drone turned itself off.

Down at the bottom, Roam 3 was busy. A loud ticking began and the cord that ran up the stairs started to tighten. And like an old lady with bad knees, Roam 3 started to pull itself up the stairs.

We screamed and shouted even louder, but it turned to

laughter as Roam 3 tipped over the edge of the first step and thumped down onto its back, like a ladybird.

"That is so lame!" cried Shannon.

"It's dead!" shouted Reggie.

"Keep the faith, kids!" said Dad.

And sure enough, the Roam 3 pulled on the cord and excruciatingly yanked itself back on course, up to the next step. Thump! It happened again. And again, and again: thirteen times to the top where it docked itself into the Winch Dock, reunited with the drone. It beeped twice as if to show how pleased it was.

"Now that's what I call a gadget," said Dad proudly.

Chapter 2
ENID'S HOUSE

TIME WITH DAD was Fun with a capital 'F'. But he wasn't always around, especially when he was working nightshifts. By the time we got up, he'd already be at work. Shannon was supposed to help us with breakfast but she was never awake in time so we helped ourself: as many Frosted Loopers or Honey Crackles as you could eat – with extra sugar if you wanted it – plus apple or orange juice swigged from the carton. Heaven.

Then Shannon would stomp downstairs, shout at us for being late, drop Reggie and me off at the school activity club and then catch the minibus to the High School down the valley.

After school we'd end up at the play park. That's where everyone went, but we usually stuck together in our gang of four: that's me, Reggie, Charlie and Izzy. Charlie is Reggie's best friend, and he always had the latest gadgets and games; Izzy is my best friend, and pretended not to like them. In fact I'm not even sure she was pretending.

We never bothered with the tiny slide and the rusty old climbing frame. Instead we huddled around Charlie's smartphone to play games and watch videos. Sometimes we'd have to hold our bags over Charlie's head to keep the

14

sun off the screen. But more often we'd catch sight of the darkening sky over the fells that surround our village and make a run for it, pushing, shoving and yelling our way home up the cul-de-sac.

When we got back, Dad was often still asleep. The only real rule in our house, the only one you never, ever broke, was Don't Wake Dad Up. So Reggie and I would creep in and take the iPad and we'd meet Charlie and Izzy back out at the front. And then we'd check that nobody was watching and push open the rusty garden gate next door.

Next door was where Enid used to live. Enid had been quite deaf, and quite, quite miserable. When she was there we could hear her telly through the wall but that meant she could hear us, too. She'd lean over the fence and thump on the front door with her walking stick. Shut those kids up, she'd say to Dad. Those kids need some discipline. They're out of control. They should be taken into care.

But although Enid hated children, she loved two things: her cat, and her plants.

Her cat was called Dudley, and she must have been about 103 years old – in real years, not cat years. Not quite black and not quite white, you'd see her out of the corner of your eye, padding along a window ledge or through the grass. She'd try to creep up on birds, and as soon as she got within five metres she'd make her move. Unfortunately her move was a half-hearted jump of about ten centimetres. Most of the time the birds wouldn't even bother flying off.

You might also have spotted that Dudley was, in fact, a

female cat. Enid wouldn't explain, and said it was none of our business. Not only that, but Dudley was a fat old girl, and as the years go on, she got fatter as Enid got thinner. "That cat is probably sucking the joy out of the old ratbag while she's asleep," said Dad.

And then there were Enid's plants. Throughout the summer her front garden would fizz with colour, a riot of tulips, begonias, petunias and snapdragons. She'd kneel on a tatty green pad with a trowel, endlessly scraping and fussing, only looking up to scowl at us when we came home.

There weren't many flowers in our garden; Dad simply strimmed it from time to time, uncovering long-lost toys and leaving clumps of choppy grass. But when Enid was living there, next door's blooms would occasionally make a bid for freedom through our fence. One time, when I was little, I sat in our empty flowerbed squeezing the heads of her snapdragons to make them talk to me. I heard a sound and looked up: Enid was *right there*, her pinched, leathery face pressed up against the slats, eyes blazing with hate. She let out a mighty squawk, a rasping cry like a pterodactyl. I ran screaming for the house. Dad went round later to complain but returned quickly, shaking his head. She's a bitter and twisted old lady, he'd said.

A bit later, when I was six, Enid became sick. Very soon a small van arrived, driven by her son. We watched from the front window as he loaded boxes into the back and his mum into the front. As he drove off there was a shriek from the passenger seat. He reversed, jumped out and pushed a mewling Dudley through the open passenger window into Enid's lap. Enid stuck out her tongue at me, and we never saw her, or Dudley, again.

The house she left behind lay empty but seemed a happier place. The grass ran riot but vigorous flowers still elbowed their way through each summer. Paint peeled and tiles slipped, but the straggly, overgrown and weather-beaten place suited us fine.

It was Charlie who discovered that her son had forgotten to lock the back door. He ran helter-skelter back to me, Reggie and Izzy, panting how he'd actually *pushed* it and it had actually *opened*. That's the way Charlie talks, by the way, like he's permanently amazed by the way the world works.

I led the way and we tiptoed through the ancient kitchen. It was tidy but dark and thick with dust. We crept cautiously into the living room. Sunlight streamed through the closed, threadbare curtains, casting a shadow of the ivy outside onto the yellowing woodchip wallpaper. A darker patch of brown carpet showed where the TV had once stood, but otherwise it was easy to imagine that Enid had just shuffled out to tend her flowers and shout at the neighbours. Charlie sat down. Clouds of dust billowed up from the sofa and we doubled up, sneezing and coughing.

Enid's house was at the end of the terrace, attached to ours. But even so, it was surprisingly different inside. Instead of having a titchy hallway like ours her front door opened straight into the lounge – or at least it had done until the door became swollen shut. That meant her stairs began in the lounge, but a locked door on the first step barred the way. We tugged and twisted, but it was shut firm.

So we were limited to the downstairs but that was OK, especially when we realised we could connect to our WiFi through the wall. Izzy brought a dustpan and brush and did her best to clean up a bit. (She's thirteen already, but sometimes I think she's fast-forwarded through the teenage years, right out the other side to where you care about things like that.) But it didn't help much – I think most of the dust left the house on our clothes as we played on the sofa or rolled on the carpet.

Did Dad know we were there? Of course he did. Even if Shannon didn't tell him, he must have realised. Once, when we said we were going out to play in the rain, he'd told us not to get wet. "Oh we won't," said Reggie in a tone that was way too clever. Dad paused, and looked at us. "Have some respect," he'd said. We knew what he meant.

One other great thing about Enid's house was that we knew exactly when Dad was waking up after a nightshift. About half past four we'd hear the toilet flushing and the creak of floorboards. That would give us enough time to pull the back door closed and run home. We'd often burst through our front door just as Dad emerged from the kitchen, holding a Strawberry Toaster Boaster and scratching his bum. And every day he'd yawn and say, "What's new, kids?" And then we'd all troop through to our lounge and the proper games session would begin.

We *loved* games in our house. Virtual reality games were the best. We climbed on the sofa and laughed at the person in the headset as they waved their arms about and bumped into the furniture. One of our favourites was one called *TV Simulator 4* where your mates went all over the house and pretended to be the presenter from war zones, hurricanes and volcanos, and you were the anchor man in the studio. And if they were rude to you then you could cut them off, or change their background from a street corner into the edge of a cliff or put them underneath a car crusher.

There was also a shooting game, a great shapes game and even a roller coaster, although we had to stop playing that one after Izzy felt a bit dizzy and had to lie down.

Before that it was all about the racing games, with a special steering wheel so you could drive your car on the TV. Reggie was the house champion; Charlie was rubbish. He crashed into the barriers, drove the wrong way around the track and lost all his game power in about three seconds. But Dad would cheer everyone on from the sofa, even jumping up and down with excitement if Charlie made it round the track without powering down. No wonder you could feel all the lumpy springs in the cushions.

But it always ended the same way – Dad would leave us to it, and rummage around in our huge chest freezer for something to eat.

"Everyone staying for tea?" he'd say, without waiting for an answer.

It wasn't a surprise for other people to turn up about then, too; everyone knew Dad worked at the frozen food factory with its factory shop selling an unlimited supply of pizzas, burgers, pies, fishfingers, ice cream and just about anything else you could freeze. One of Shannon's mates would pop their head around the open back door and make up some excuse about needing to borrow some clothes or a school book, but their roving eyes gave the game away.

"We're having our tea right now," Dad would say. "Have you had yours yet?"

"Not yet, Mr Batty."

(They always called Dad "Mr Batty". That was his real name, of course, but even though he told them to call him John, they carried on being extra polite in case it got them an extra helping.)

"No tea yet, Mr Batty. I think Mum is a bit busy. What are those?"

"They're Flash-Fried Fishy Feet. Try saying that 10 times quickly. You'll see them in the shops soon, they'll be everywhere. Would you like to try one?"

"Ooh yes please, Mr Batty." And our visitor would flop into the kitchen and sit down at the kitchen table, grinning.

"Here you go. A couple of fishy feet and a few spare chips. Send your mum a message, let her know you're here." And Dad would deliver a mountain of food, because he always cooked too much, 'just in case'.

And that's how it was: a house full of games, gadgets and goofing around, topped off with mountains of chips. But it wasn't going to stay that way. We didn't know it, but The Changes were around the corner. Sure, we noticed the *little* changes, but none of us joined the dots. None of us took a step back to see the big picture, work out what was going on. Not until it was too late, anyway.

Would it have made any difference? Could we have put the brakes on? Could we have ganged up together with some other kids, like a junior rebel alliance?

Probably not. What could kids do against a force that strong? But at least we would have put up a proper fight. Instead we were herded like sheep, driven bleating into a pen. Only then did we look up and find the world looking back, watching and pointing.

Chapter 3
MELISSA

"DINNER'S READY!"

Melissa was standing at the bottom of the stairs. She was now wearing jeans, and looked much better: more normal, even a bit like a mum. You could tell she was still new, though, and a bit posh, because she called it dinner instead of tea.

For once, it was nearly as good as Dad's. Melissa had put cheese and breadcrumbs on pasta and put it under the grill until it was golden, bubbly and crunchy. "I was going to do a salad," she said as we sat down, "but it seems you've run out of vegetables. Or anything green. Or anything fresh." She looked at Dad sternly, though her eyes twinkled.

"I *am* surprised," said Dad, not looking surprised at all. "I think maybe the rabbits ate it all." We don't have any rabbits. Never have.

Dad put his phone on the table but she reached out and took it, placing it into the fruit bowl alongside her own. "You too, Shannon," she said, holding out the bowl. "New rule for mealtimes."

Shannon looked at Dad, who shrugged. Reggie and I grinned: we didn't have our own phones. Shannon scowled and harrumphed, but dropped her phone in. During the meal the fruit bowl sometimes buzzed or pinged. Dad or Shannon looked over, or at each other, but neither of them dared get up to check.

We still weren't used to mealtimes with Melissa, to be honest. Before she arrived there had been five long years when it was just Dad, Shannon, Reggie and me.

That's five years without Rose Marie Batty, aged 38. Rosie, as everyone called her. Rosie, mother of Thora (that's me), and Reggie (that's my brother), and step mum to Shannon. Rosie, who took a taxi to hospital to have her tonsils removed and never came home.

Five years since Rosie's photo was in the local paper, her arm wrapped round Dad at a wedding, above the headline: *Teacher's shock death prompts hospital enquiry.*

Five years of questions, and stares, and people saying *poor you,* and *it must be **so** tough.*

Four years since Dad heard the experts decide that it was just really, really bad luck she died. That an infection she could have caught anywhere had caught her instead, and wouldn't let her go.

Three years since Dad burst into tears again during tea, when Shannon said it wasn't *her* mum who died so she didn't have to care and Dad thumped the wall and we all started crying and Shannon ran screaming from the room.

Two years since he finally smiled when Reggie asked him to tell a 'Mummy story'. Since he got a promotion at the frozen food factory.

One year since he set up his online dating profile.

And six months since Shannon found out, and he allowed her to rewrite it and take control of his life.

Melissa was Shannon's pick, of course. Dad and Shannon spent hours together, sat at the kitchen table after Reggie and I were supposed to be in bed, swiping through the options.

Dad squinted at a profile pic. "She looks alright."

"Her? She looks like she's chewing a wasp," Shannon replied.

"What about that one?"

"You're joking. She'd eat you alive and ask for seconds."

"What about her? She looks lovely."

"You'd be lucky, Dad, she looks like a supermodel."

"Yeah, fair enough," Dad sighed. "In any case, she's probably not even real. Or she's a long distance lorry driver called Malcolm."

"OK then," said Dad, after a pause. "What about this one?"

"She's a bit out of your league, too," said Shannon. I peered over her shoulder to look at the picture of a slim, serious-looking woman standing on a beach in a wetsuit. "Nice hair. And if she can afford to go diving in a place like that, she must be minted."

"Sounds like a perfect match," said Dad. "I reckon I'd look pretty hot in a wetsuit."

"Sweaty, you mean," I said.

Dad noticed me for the first time. "Hey, look at that. A free insult with every daughter. Go to bed." I took no notice.

"Hmm," said Shannon. She was zooming in on the image. "Quite a few wrinkles. I reckon she's older than you. You might stand a chance, then."

"Charming. Go on then, Cupid. Send her an email she can't resist. Tell her I'll meet her outside the International Space Station at six, or at the Chinese restaurant in town at eight, whatever works best."

And that's how it started. With a shirt ironed badly by Dad and then better by Shannon, and new shoes that he said rubbed on his big toe, he caught the 101 bus from the village green into town.

The following day at tea, Shannon didn't waste any time. "You got back early last night. Did you stuff it up then?"

"Nope," smiled Dad. "Or at least I don't think so. She's working on a big project, so she had to get back to her hotel to do some slides."

"Doesn't sound very promising. Or interesting."

"Did you kiss her?" Reggie had asked as he gnawed on a Sticky Toffee Rib.

Dad grinned.

"You did!" shrieked Shannon. "You absolute tart."

"Now, now," said Dad. "A gentleman should never kiss and tell. Anyway, she's nice. Friendly. You'll like her."

"You've invited her here already?"

"Yep, next weekend," said Dad, through a mouthful of sticky ribs. "She's getting a taxi around lunchtime."

Shannon dropped her knife on the plate with a clatter. "O.M.G. You do know it's Valentine's Day, right? She's after something. She's a bunny boiler."

"She boils bunnies?" asked Reggie, looking excited.

"Take no notice," said Dad. "She's far too intelligent, but obviously she finds me irresistible. And besides, she hasn't got anywhere else to go because all her friends live down south, and she's staying up this way for the weekend because of work or something."

"I take it back," said Shannon. "You're a perfect match: she's demented and you're desperate."

He waved his fork at me. "I'm taking no notice. The path of true love stretches out before me. Pass me the laptop, Thora. Time to change my relationship status."

And that was all Dad had to do: tap an icon. But what about *my* relationship status?

Because in a few weeks Reggie and I went from being kids-with-a-mum-who-died, to kids with Melissa who definitely wasn't our mum, but spent pretty much every weekend acting like one. Cooking, talking to Dad, taking us to the park, stuff like that. She'd turn up late on Friday night and let herself in if Dad was on a nightshift. Or she'd arrive on Thursday instead, and we'd find her tapping away on her laptop at the kitchen table in her running gear when we got home from school.

She wasn't Shannon's mum either, of course. That would be Rachel. When Dad and Rachel split up, long before I was born, Rachel went back to New Zealand where she had grown up. But that's as much as I can tell you because I've never met her, she doesn't have FaceTime and she doesn't use a computer. Maybe Shannon was in touch with her, maybe not: we weren't allowed to ask her about it.

So Melissa, the new girl, was not-a-mum to all of us. But only Shannon made that *crystal* clear.

25

"What's for pudding?" Reggie asked. He'd finished his cheesy pasta already.

"A big dollop of fresh air I'm afraid, mister," said Dad. "I got there too late. Gloria from IT bought all the ice cream for a Brownies sleepover."

"It's no bad thing anyway," said Melissa. "It's a myth that you need a pudding after every meal. No wonder this country's got such a problem with childhood obesity."

"You could have bought it at a shop like normal people," said Shannon, ignoring Melissa.

"Have you seen their prices?" said Dad.

"Well maybe we wouldn't need to buy our food from a factory shop if there wasn't an extra mouth to feed," muttered Shannon into her plate.

Melissa and Dad froze, like a YouTube video on pause. Gravy dribbled off Dad's fork. Melissa started to speak, but Dad held his hand up. His chair squawked on the tile floor as he slowly got to his feet, watched by Shannon out of the corner of her eye.

"Well," he said in a dangerously calm voice. "I guess there is one easy way we could free up a bit of budget."

He crossed over to the blackboard on the kitchen wall where Dad kept track of Shannon's allowance, because she was always asking for an advance. The figures £40, £30 and £25 were already crossed out. Licking his fingertip, Dad drew a line through the remaining £20. "There we go, Reggie," he said, but looking directly at Shannon. "Sorted. You choose the flavour, I'll pick it up from the supermarket."

Shannon's chair clattered backwards onto the floor. Dad sighed and sat down as she slammed the kitchen door and stomped up the stairs.

"I'd like chocolate and strawberry and vanilla please, Daddy," said Reggie in a quiet voice. Dad reached over with a smile and ruffled his hair.

"That girl," sighed Dad, "what are we going to do with her?" He picked up a spare rib and popped it in his mouth. He chewed for a moment, and then his face brightened. "I wonder if I could flog her on eBay?'

Chapter 4
QUESTIONS, QUESTIONS

EVEN THOUGH MELISSA had been staying the night more often it was still a shock when I found her waiting outside school, dressed for a run. Reggie was careering around as usual, pretending to be a character from his favourite video game, *Ogre Smackdown*. Melissa waved.

"Hi Thora. Did you have a good day?"

"Hi. Why are you here?"

"I fancied a bit of fresh air, so I said I'd come. You don't mind, do you?"

'S'pose not."

I did mind, in fact. Everyone would see her and tomorrow they'd be asking me all about her, crowding round and wanting answers. Answers I didn't have.

I grabbed my rucksack. "Can we go to the play park?"

It was a bright, blowy day, the sort that looks warm through the classroom window but makes your ears sting with cold before you've reached the gate. Clouds skidded across the valley and a rippling patchwork of sunlight and shadow flickered across the steep face of the fells.

We walked quickly across the playground and out to the crossing, our gang of four plus Izzy's and Charlie's mums. And Melissa, of course, though she walked behind, on her own. We stamped our feet and chatted while curly-haired Sheila, in her day-glow yellow safety jacket, crossed slowly to the centre of the road carrying her battered old lollipop sign.

"Got a date for that hip operation yet, Sheila?" asked Izzy's mum as we passed.

"Yes, dear – should be done by Christmas. You watch, I'll be doing cartwheels by spring!"

And with that she painfully inched her way back to the kerb while we skipped on down the road, through the swing gate and into the park.

Charlie was flavour of the month at school because he had a supercharged new tablet and preloaded games pack. His mum brought it with her – we weren't allowed devices in class. The boys huddled near the climbing frame, shouting excitedly whenever someone got a high score.

Izzy and I found a sheltered corner near the swings where she could show me Instagrams of her cousin in Australia. Only it turns out that her cousin wasn't taking selfies by the pool, or hanging out with boys or anything like that; instead she was showing the world her favourite maths problems on a whiteboard.

"You're not going to get many likes for stuff like that," I said.

"I've already written up the equations into my maths project book," said Izzy. (It's worth pointing out that there's no such thing as a maths project book at our school, unless you're Izzy.) "I'm showing them to Mrs Hooper tomorrow lunchtime. She's going to love them." Mrs Hooper is in charge of maths.

"That's not a real like, Izzy."

"It's better than a *like*, it's an actual *love*," said Izzy, flicking her hair.

I sighed.

"Reggie, Thora, let's go!" shouted Melissa into the wind after about five minutes. She'd been sitting on the roundabout waiting for us, some distance from the other mums. The real mums, I mean.

I said goodbye to Izzy and her crazy maths problems and joined Melissa.

"Don't you ever play games on the field?" she asked as we walked home.

"Like what?"

"Well, like tag, or hide and seek, or – "

"That's what we do at school," said Reggie. "*This* is when we get to do what we want."

"But you must get bored, standing around, looking at those... *devices*." She said the word 'devices' like it tasted nasty.

I looked at Reggie, and we both shrugged. "Nope," I said. "And if we had our own phones we wouldn't need to look at theirs."

A thought struck Reggie. When that happens he virtually wags his tail in excitement. "Will *you* get us one? Please?"

"Not a chance," said Melissa. "But anytime you want to come out for a run with me, I'm all yours."

"Not likely," I said. "I can always go round to Izzy's anyway. Her Dad's got a treadmill with a screen attached so you can jog and play chess at the same time."

"Isn't the world a marvellous place," murmured Melissa, giving our sticky front gate a shove.

I got the feeling Melissa wouldn't be picking us up again any time soon.

After I'd changed I padded downstairs in my slippers and found Melissa in the lounge, standing in front of HOUSE 2.0. I should explain: HOUSE 2.0 was Dad's big project. Three years after Mum died he had sketched the outline of a huge house in pencil on the wall, filling the space from floor to ceiling. It was a house like a five-year-old would draw: four windows, a door, a roof with a chimney and a picket fence around the outside. Above the house he'd glued big capital letters from a magazine: HOUSE 2.0.

And then gradually, oh-so-slowly, he'd started to draw each section in ink, and fill in the details. He did it late at night, after we were asleep. The outline was the first to be inked in, followed by a window. Then, over the following months, he started to furnish the room inside with detailed sketches: a toilet and a sink, followed by flowery wallpaper and a lampshade. Outside he'd started to add guttering, pipes and a chimney pot.

This house didn't exist, of course: not in our village, or down in the town, or anywhere. But it would. It was a concept, Dad said, a family project. Our real house seemed to be shrinking by the week. Shannon's room was tiny anyway. And with all our stuff in it, the front bedroom that Reggie and I shared was pretty cramped too. So Dad was saving for somewhere bigger, somewhere new. And when the drawing was complete, when all the lines were solid and all the rooms were full, we'd have saved enough money

31

and we could move and buy somewhere like HOUSE 2.0.

The problem was clear: he wasn't saving fast enough. I'd be 80 by the time it was ready. If this were a real house it would have no roof, nowhere to sleep, and the toilet would flush out of a hole in the wall. Almost nothing changed from week to week so that HOUSE 2.0 had literally become wallpaper: something to ignore when you were watching telly.

Melissa was standing in front of it, tracing her finger over the wispy pencil lines. I stood behind her. "He isn't doing very well, is he?"

Melissa almost jumped out of her skin. "Goodness, Thora! You almost gave me a heart attack. Anyway, he's doing his best."

"He needs to rob a bank or something."

"I'm not sure your father is a bank robbing kind of man," said Melissa. "He'd probably get caught in his getaway car playing with the satnav."

"Maybe he'll get another promotion, what with his employee award and everything."

"Maybe," said Melissa, steering me towards the stairs. "Now get yourself changed and come downstairs, I'll make you a snack."

I did what she said, but I had a funny feeling I knew what was coming next, because she'd done it before. I was right. She lured me into the kitchen with celery and carrot sticks and then BAM! She hit me with a quick-fire quiz. Dad said she wanted to get to know us a bit better, and she certainly wasn't afraid to ask the questions. Although Shannon wasn't answering any of them, so perhaps I got her share too.

That day, her chosen topic was Leisure. What did I like to do? (Play video games.) What was my favourite game? (*Race Max 2*.) What was my favourite game but not on the computer? (I couldn't think of one.) How often did my friends come over to play? (Every day.) How many friends did I have? (One, plus Charlie but he didn't really count.) What time did I get to bed? (I told her 9 o'clock.) What was my favourite TV programme? (Robo Avengers, but I preferred YouTube.) Who chose the channel? (The biggest person in the room.)

Reggie came into the kitchen, made a face at the selection of snacks on offer, and walked right into her trap. He reached for a carrot. She pounced. What music did he like? What videos had he seen? What websites did he visit most? How many apps did he know? When did he do his homework?

"In the playground before school," Reggie had said in answer to that last question, through a shower of carrot pieces. That had surprised her a little. But it was true: Reggie might say and do some daft things, but there's a big brain in there somewhere. He just needs to turn it on.

Dad has always said that the worst people he meets at work are the ones who never ask questions, because it means they're only interested in themselves. So in case Melissa thought the same thing, I tried a couple of questions too, as soon as I could get a word in.

Where did she live? In a terraced house in a small Sussex village.

On her own? Yes. She used to be married, to an engineer, but he died in an accident a long time ago.

Where did she work? In London, for the government.

So why was she up here? Was she a spy? (That one was Reggie.) No, of course not. Just a civil servant, and they work all over the country on different things.

What were her hobbies? Running. (As if I hadn't guessed.) Diving. (I didn't tell her I knew that, too, from her profile pic.) Reading. (Books, mostly, not websites.)

Was she going to marry Dad? (Reggie again.) No answer on that one, but she blushed and decided that was enough questions for now.

Maybe that last question put an idea into her head, though. Later that night I woke up needing a wee. I crossed the landing and for once I didn't stub my toe on the Winch Dock, which was still strapped to the banisters.

Downstairs I could hear the telly: it was the unmistakable haw-haw voice of the new Prime Minister. He was blathering on about a "return to family values", "healthy bodies and healthy minds", "a fresh start for the nation's youth" and other words that have plenty of sound but no meaning. He had been on TV every day since the election last month, on every channel, trying to get people to like him. But that was hard for lots of reasons: he had replaced a nice, normal woman who hadn't done much, but hadn't upset anyone either; he had been caught on camera using a wet wipe to clean his hands after he'd picked up a baby on a visit to a pre-school; and he looked like a ripe tomato about to explode.

I was about to walk into the bathroom when I heard Melissa say something from the kitchen.

"I can't hear you!" Dad shouted back, before flicking off the TV. "That's better. I know he's basically your boss and everything, but that man gets up my nose."

"I've never even met him. I'm really not that important," said Melissa. "But some of his ideas are sound." Her voice got louder as she came out into the hall; I ducked back into the darkened bathroom. "So... have you then?"

"Have I what?" asked Dad.

"Have you thought about my idea?"

"Uh-huh."

"You should. It's definitely worth thinking about."

Dad was quiet; perhaps he was thinking. Melissa returned to the kitchen. A teaspoon tinkled in a mug. The swing bin went flump. "I feel like you're pushing me into it. It would be a big change," he said eventually.

"I didn't mean it that way. But it would be a change for the better, surely," said Melissa, crossing the hall with two mugs of tea. "We can't go on the same, none of us can, it's not working. And opportunities like this... I'm asking you because it's a great idea, but also because it could be the start of something really big for all of us."

Crikey. I wondered if they'd get married in our tiny village church, or maybe back where Melissa comes from.

I heard Dad shuffle on the sofa. "Don't get me wrong, I like the idea. And who wouldn't say yes, with that dangled in front of you. But..." Dad paused, and coughed. "Since Rosie died, I haven't had much choice: the kids have been left to their own devices. But they seem happy enough, don't they?"

"They're happy, and they're a credit to you. But can't you see what they're missing?" Melissa sounded excited now. "This could be your chance – *our* chance – to give them that back. And we'd take it slowly. I've done my homework. I can use my influence. And we'd be doing it together. And if they don't like it we could always – "

But then the old dishwasher started to gurgle and slosh, and despite me straining so hard to hear I thought I'd burst, the rest was burble.

Interesting. Maybe Dad's dating profile would need *another* update.

Chapter 5
PARENTS EVENING

AT SCHOOL, THE Easter holidays were definitely on the way. Times tables and handwriting practice were out. Toy Story DVDs and extra playtime were in.

Parents Evening rolled around, too. It was the usual routine: Mrs Scott told Dad I was doing well academically, but I needed to be more confident in my own abilities and wouldn't I like to join a club like drama or debating? What, and be stared at by a bazillion people? No thanks, Mrs Scott.

We found Reggie in the corner of the hall playing games with Charlie on his mum's smartphone and dragged my brother to the other end of the school to meet his teacher, Mr Richards.

In some ways, Reggie was completely normal. He did all the revolting things that eight-year-old boys do. Farts, burps, picking his nose, calling me names, that kind of thing. He was fearless and was always getting his best friend Charlie into trouble because Reggie was skinny and brainy while Charlie... well, Charlie wasn't either of those things. Cheeky and afraid of nothing: that was School Reggie.

But Home Reggie wasn't always like that. Home Reggie was much smaller, just a short-haired, freckly boy without a Mum, really. He didn't remember Mum at all, so for years we shared my ragged, picked-over memories instead. If we saw a girl being carried on her mum's shoulders, he'd point and say, "That's like our Mummy used to do with you, isn't it Thora?" Or he'd eat his tea and say "Cheese on toast is our favourite because Mummy liked it, didn't she Thora?" And I'd look up and find him by my side, leaning into me, thumb in his mouth.

But this was parents evening, so School Reggie was out to play. It was the last slot of the night, just a few stragglers wandering the corridors. At the door to Reggie's classroom a gangly, spider of a man wearing a Visitor badge and clutching an iPad was chatting to Reggie's teacher. All arms and legs, he had folded himself into the doorway with his head on an angle, nearly bumping the frame. He noticed us and straightened up in the corridor, reaching his full height somewhere up near the lightbulbs.

"Good evening," he said as he passed us, taking us both by surprise with his deep, plummy voice.

"Hello," I said.

"Good evening," said Reggie, doing his best imitation. The man smiled thinly and was gone.

Dad gave Reggie a light wallop on the shoulder. "Zip it, cheeky. Come on, let's hear what Mr Richards has to say. Hang tight here, Thora, we'll be out in ten minutes." And he gave Reggie a shove into the classroom.

When they came out Dad summed it up in the usual way: could try harder. He talked about how Reggie should spend less time playing games and more time on his homework. And Reggie nodded, and said "Yes Dad!", and we all knew he would take no notice.

"Shannon should be here somewhere to pick you up," said Dad as we neared the hall.

"Why aren't we coming home with you?" said Reggie.

"The parents need to stay on for a meeting," said Dad. "I'll be home in a bit."

Sure enough Shannon was there, tapping away on her phone, but we were lucky to spot her. Instead of emptying out, the school was filling up: mums and dads were spilling through the doors and into the hall, which was already three-quarters full and buzzing with chatter and laughter. Through a gap in the crowd I even saw someone who looked like Melissa, talking to a mum on the front row. But my view was soon obstructed, and I couldn't be sure.

"What's the meeting about?" Reggie asked.

"Oh, some government nonsense," said Dad, waving to Shannon. "Changes in the National Curriculum, I think."

"What's eff-eff?" said Reggie, pointing to a sign on the wall with the letters FF squashed inside a circle, and an arrow pointing to the hall.

"I dunno," said Dad, bending to give us a kiss. "Something instantly forgettable, I'm sure. Fast Forward? Food Fight? Fat Fingers? Something like that. Right kids, get out of here!"

Following Shannon we bundled our way through the main doors and out into the night.

The next morning I was woken just after dawn by the sound of Dad getting ready for work: he was back on day shifts. The buzz of his electric toothbrush. A bit of grunting as he pulled on his trousers, and a thud as he toppled into the wall while putting his socks on. The soft *whumph!* as he let the fridge door slam shut, a carton of Chocca Mocca Moo Moo Milk in hand ready for his breakfast on the go. A clunk as the front door closed, and then the sound of our elderly car being nagged back to life.

(Dad always drove to work. Last year he'd been given a 21-speed mountain bike by the factory for 'outstanding service'. Shannon had laughed like a hyena when he pulled that out of the car boot. After remarking that he'd need a jet engine strapped to the back to get up the steep valley road from the factory, Dad shoved it into the shed and that's the last time we saw it.)

As the sound of Dad's car faded I held my breath so I could breathe out at the same time as Reggie. In, out, pause. In, out, pause. When I got it right, I could no longer tell us apart.

The distant hiss of the first bus into town broke the spell, and I realised I needed a wee. I hopped out of bed. Grey morning light seeped into the room through the curtains, enough for me to see my way to the door.

On the landing I instinctively lifted my foot to clear the Winch Dock. I'd learnt my lesson the painful way. But on the return journey the bathroom door was open. A shaft of sunlight from the window struck the landing floor, and at first I didn't even notice what wasn't there. At the foot of the bannisters was a patch of blue carpet which was much cleaner than its surroundings, ironically. The Winch Dock – home to Dad's prize and joy, his best new gadget – had disappeared.

Chapter 6
SENSORS WORKING OVERTIME

"I SOLD IT," Dad said through a mouthful of Chicken Chiplets. "Stuck it on eBay. The app was rubbish, it couldn't clean the corners, and the drone nearly took my head off. Still, I reckon we got a chimney out of it," said Dad, gesturing with his fork towards the lounge. I craned my neck, and sure enough HOUSE 2.0 had a new inked addition.

"Now then, while I remember. Shannon, can you keep an ear out for the doorbell in the morning, around half past seven?"

"Don't worry John, I'll be here to let them in," said Melissa quickly.

"Let who in?" I asked.

Melissa looked at Dad.

"We're getting an alarm system fitted," said Dad.

Shannon looked up. "Who'd nick anything from this dump?"

"That's not very nice, Shannon. There's the telly for starters. Then there's the, erm, games console. And – "

"There's lots of things," interrupted Melissa. "It's

common sense. Plenty of people in the village are getting it done because there's a new government grant."

The last time I'd seen a police car in our village had been two years before, when they'd driven up from town to give Jade Smith a telling off. She'd nicked some stuff from the shop on the green. There's one road in, one road out, everyone's a nosy neighbour and nobody drives a Rolls Royce. Not the place I'd choose to start a crime wave.

But sure enough the doorbell rang as we were having breakfast next morning. Reggie jumped up but Melissa beat him to it. Three men stood on the doorstep in crinkly white boiler suits, looking like a forensic team arriving at the scene of a crime.

Melissa and the men huddled on the drive, talking quietly.

"An hour, yeah?" I heard one of the men say. Melissa nodded and they got back into their van. It was the plainest, whitest and cleanest van you've ever seen, except for a red spot the size of a tennis ball, low down on the side.

"Where have they gone?" asked Reggie.

"They'll be back soon. It'll be easier for them to start when you're out at school," said Melissa. "Now get a move on, we're running late."

When we got home that afternoon Melissa was on the doorstep. One of the alarm installers appeared from the lounge with a toolbox. "Right, all done," he said. "See you soon."

He walked down our drive to his van, nodding at me

as we passed. The other two men were waiting in the passenger seat, drinking pop.

"Oh, hi!" said Melissa brightly. "Did you kids enjoy your day?" She didn't wait for an answer. "That was good timing. They've just finished."

The van driver started the engine.

"Why did he say 'see you soon'? Is he coming back?" I asked.

"No," said Melissa. "It was a turn of phrase."

"I wouldn't bet on it," I said. "They've gone the wrong way."

Sure enough we heard the van turning round at the end of the cul-de-sac, and a moment later it whizzed back past us. On the back, at the bottom of the doors, was another red spot.

Back inside the house I couldn't see any changes. But Shannon did. She walked to the end of the hall and looked up.

"What's *that?*" she said, pointing. As she did so, a red light flashed inside a shiny silver-grey object, about the size of a satsuma. It was mounted on a stalk that poked out of the corner.

"It looks like a bug eye," said Reggie.

"It looks like a camera for shoplifters," said Shannon.

"It's no such thing," said Melissa. "It's a motion sensor, checking if there's anyone in the room. Look!" And she started doing star jumps with a grin on her face. "Come on Reggie, give it a go! It's such great fun!"

"No thanks," said Reggie, walking into the kitchen.

Shannon hadn't moved. "I don't like it," she said finally.

"Well... " said Melissa, turning her palms outwards.

She smiled at me, though I'm not sure why. Probably because I was the only person who hadn't been rude to her.

Shannon walked into the lounge. "There's one in here, too!" she shouted.

"And here," replied Reggie from the kitchen, through a mouthful of crisps.

"That's right," said Melissa, taking the packet out of Reggie's hands. "It wouldn't be any good if we only had one, would it?"

Shannon came charging out of the lounge and ran up the stairs to her room. "And here! They're everywhere!"

"How does it know if we're a robber, or if we're supposed to be here?" I asked.

"It knows if the house is supposed to be empty," said Melissa.

"How?"

"Computers. Artificial Intelligence. Because it learns when we go to work and school, and when we're asleep. And if it spots something unusual, it sends an alert out."

"Who to?"

"To your Daddy."

"And then Daddy drives home really fast," said Shannon sarcastically, leaning over the bannisters, "as long as he can get the car started, and knocks the robbers out with a box of frozen chicken wings."

Melissa did a little *fnumph* noise, as if to say 'well, if you're going to be like that,' and sat down in front of her laptop at the kitchen table.

"You're getting yourself worked up over nothing," said Dad at dinner. Melissa had gone back to her hotel, saying she'd got a bunch of work to do and it would be easier to concentrate there.

"I just don't get why everyone suddenly needs burglar alarms," said Shannon, grabbing the ketchup. "Zoe texted me, she's had one fitted. So has Alice, and Tara."

"It's like Mimi said about the grants –"

"Wait, *Mimi?*" said Shannon, a smile spreading across her face. "Who's Mimi? Since when has *Melissa* become a *Mimi?*"

Dad blushed. "It's only a nickname. I'm sure you can call her that too, if you want."

"I might," said Shannon, "just to embarrass you."

"It won't work," said Dad, blushing. "I'm not easily embarrassed."

"Nah," said Shannon. "I'll stick with Melissa. She's your girlfriend, not mine."

"Mimi and Daddy, sitting in a tree," I chanted. Reggie joined in, shouting. "K-I-S-S-I-N –"

"Pack it in, you two!"

"I reckon she's got you hook, line and sinker," said Shannon. "She must *really* like Porky Parcels and Chicken Stripzers."

"Who doesn't?" said Dad. "They're the world's finest frozen fancy food, it says so on the packet."

There was a knock at the back door. Shannon's friend Alice walked straight in and sat down at the table.

"Sorry I'm late," she said. "Mum was explaining how the alarm system works."

Dad raised his eyebrows at Shannon.

"Oh yes," she said. "I forgot to mention, I invited Alice over to tea. That's OK, isn't it, Dad?"

Dad got to his feet, giving Shannon a punch on the arm as he walked over to the oven.

"Ow!"

"Of course, Alice, you're very welcome. Shannon was telling me how I'm the best dad in the world. Feel free to agree if you'd like some tea."

After we'd finished, Shannon took Alice to her room and the rest of us played *Race Max 2* until it became obvious that nobody was about to beat Reggie's high score of three and a half million.

"Right, come on both of you, time for bed," said Dad.

But as I followed them out of the room, something caught my eye. "Dad!" I called.

"What's up?" called Dad from half way up the stairs.

"Have you got a new job or something?" I stood and stared at HOUSE 2.0. The roof and walls were now outlined in solid ink. The outside of the house was complete.

"I wish," said Dad. "Teeth, Reggie! I've told you three times already! Why d'you ask, Thora?"

"It's... HOUSE 2.0..." There was a pause. "Dad?"

"Oh, that. I got a bit more for the Roam 3 than I thought," Dad said from upstairs. "Now come on, get your PJs on at least."

I wasn't sure how much walls and a new roof could cost. But could it really be the same as a vacuum cleaner? Even the world's first drone-operated one?

Chapter 7
MR WHARTON

IT WAS THE last day of the spring term.

In assembly, after the usual prize giving, our head teacher Mr Frost held up his hands to make an announcement.

"Before you disappear and bury your heads in an Easter Egg, we have one last special visitor to talk to you," he said. He grinned, white teeth flashing in his perma-tanned face, like he does when he's about to make a joke he likes. "Some of you may have seen him before. He's got big floppy ears, he likes carrots and there's a rumour he lives underground... yes, it's Mr Wharton!"

The reception children laughed at Frosty's joke – they'll laugh at anything – and a few teachers rolled their eyes.

Mr Wharton had been standing to one side in every assembly we'd had since parents evening, sometimes tapping away on his iPad, but always looking pale-faced and serious, like he was at a funeral. Mr Wharton now took to the stage and held out his hands for quiet, though nobody was talking anyway.

"Boys and girls," he said in his deep, booming voice. "What I'm about to show you will shock you to the core."

Now he had our attention.

"Reception children, I'd like 20% of you to stand up."

The little children looked at each other and laughed. Some of them stood up and sat straight back down again. Frosty nipped back on stage and whispered in Mr Wharton's ear.

"Yes, yes, of course. Silly me. Let's try something else. Right then, would everyone with... brown hair in reception stand up!"

About half of the class stood up, including some who didn't know what hair colour they had.

"No, no, this isn't working. Can somebody help me out here, please?" He looked to Mrs Bentley, the reception teacher.

"Sit down, Rabbits class, and only stand up if I tap you on the head." She bopped the nearest six kids, who all stood up.

"Thank you. Right then, it's your turn, Year Seven. You should be old enough. Starting over by the doors, I want every third person to stand up."

I looked behind me, and it was like a bad game of musical chairs with children standing up, sitting down and then standing up again. But eventually they worked it out.

"Right!" said Mr Wharton, looking very pleased with himself. "You have to imagine that this hall full of children is, in fact, our whole country. And here's that shocking news I was talking about: everyone standing up is *overweight* or *obese!*"

Well, we couldn't stop laughing at that, at least at first. Everyone started pointing at the children standing up, and lots of the boys started mucking around, sticking out their tummies and blowing out their cheeks.

But then, before Mr Frost could intervene, children

48

started to stop each other, saying "Shh!" to the ones who were clowning around and "Stop it! Look!" Because two children in my year – Eloise and Stanley – had tears running down their face. And so did many of the reception children, who really didn't understand why their friends were pointing at them and saying rude things.

Mr Frost called out from the sidelines. "Time to move on, Mr Wharton. Sit down please, children."

Mr Wharton looked out at a silent hall. He didn't look in the least bit sorry. "I think that proves my point," he said. "So why *are* so many children in this country overweight?"

A howl rose up from Eloise, who ran into the arms of Mrs Brown, the Year Seven teacher. Mr Wharton ignored her.

A child at the front nervously put up his hand.

"Yes?"

"They... eat too much?"

"That's right! They Eat Too Much. But there's more to it than that, isn't there? What else? Yes, you at the back."

"They eat chips and things?"

"Well done, girl! These children are fat because they are eating *unhealthily*."

Another wail, this time from a reception child.

"Oh for goodness sake," said Mr Wharton irritably. "Not you specifically, children, I'm talking generally. Do keep up." It seemed unlikely that Mr Wharton had ever been to teacher training school.

"Here's another question. How many of you eat 5 fruit or vegetables each day? Come along, hands up!"

This one was easy; we'd heard all about this in class. Tentatively, looking at each other, nearly everyone raised their hand. I thought for a moment and decided I'd rather hide in the crowd than be one of the only children with their hands down.

Mr Wharton paused. "Right. I want everyone who *doesn't* have their hand in the air to stand up. Everybody else, hands down."

A dozen children got nervously to their feet – including Charlie and Reggie, I noticed. All of them looked like they were regretting their honesty.

"Well done!" said Mr Wharton triumphantly. "You are the only children in this hall that I believe! Fewer than five? Yes! I expect so! Now do something about it, before it's too late. Sit down, you've probably not got the strength to stand much longer in any case."

Mr Wharton strode around the stage. "Now then, as for the rest of you – well you're not fooling me and you're likely not fooling yourself! If you were French children, God forbid, then your target would be 10 pieces per day! Ten! So you have a *lot* of work to do."

Mr Frost interrupted. "Have you finished, Mr Wharton?"

"Not quite. Because there's another villain I want to talk about."

We all looked around, wondering who would be next for group humiliation.

"Please can I ask the male teachers to stand up and indulge my little exercise," said Mr Wharton with a half smile.

Our four male teachers looked at each other, but got to their feet.

"Now then..." Mr Wharton squinted at the teachers,

looking them up and down and pointing at each of them in turn. "Left pocket, left pocket, right pocket, left pocket. Empty them, please. They looked at Mr Frost, who nodded. And then each pulled out their mobile phone.

"There! There we have it! Those screens are the reason that a quarter of adults are officially inactive, and thousands of children spend more than six hours a day sitting on their bottoms every weekend!"

I noticed that Mr Wharton didn't have his iPad with him today.

"I'm taking it for granted that none of you children want to end up fat and miserable," said Mr Wharton, "which is why we're going to make your lives a little easier, and tastier this holiday. Your teachers will be giving you each an activity pack, full of splendid games that you'll find are far more fun than your tablets and so forth. And we've also been talking to your parents about how you can eat more healthily, too. I think that it's safe to say we can expect some big improvements at Rain & Shine Academy. And rest assured we'll be watching – *observing* your progress, and indeed cheering you on from the sidelines, won't we Mr Frost?"

"Yes, quite," said Mr Frost, getting swiftly from his seat. "We've run out of time so thank you very much, Mr Wharton, for your most *informative* talk. And children, we'll have some exciting new developments on this subject straight after the Easter holidays. Right, everyone back to class!'

Chapter 8
BIG BROWN ENVELOPES

SHORTLY BEFORE HOME time Mrs Scott handed out our big padded activity envelopes.

"Don't open these until you get home, children. And now I have one final Easter surprise for you," she said, raising her voice to be heard. "No homework this Easter – you all deserve a break. I want you to have fun instead."

Sounds of amazement quickly turned to cheers.

Izzy put her hand up.

Mrs Scott gestured for quiet. "What is it, Izzy?"

"That's not normal, Miss. Are you *sure* there's no homework?"

Everyone groaned, but Izzy took no notice. She doesn't care what people think.

"I'm absolutely certain," said Mrs Scott. "See your friends, run around like Mr Wharton said, try not to scrape your knees." She opened the door. "You can say that's your homework if you like, Izzy."

Izzy grinned. "Yes Miss, I will!"

We sprinted out of the door, loaded down with book bags, models, bulging rucksacks and PE kits.

"Happy Easter!" Reggie yelled at Sheila as we ran across the road, and Sheila grinned and gave her lollipop a little twirl. And in the park we barely had time for phone games as we told each other our holiday plans.

"I'm going to Laser Chase," Charlie told Reggie. "We're getting the bus and I'm going to laser my brother's head off and get 1000 points."

"Oh! That sounds brilliant. I wish I could come. Hey, get your mum to download the app," said Reggie, who knows all about these things. "I saw it on telly. You get a free Coke."

"Show me how to do it, Reggie," said Charlie, handing over his tablet. He checked to make sure his mum couldn't hear him and grinned. "I know her password."

Izzy swished her straight brown hair. "I'm going to the Museum of Science. On the train." Izzy is a bit like that – she'd rather do something that feels like homework, even when there isn't any. "What will you be doing?"

"I dunno," I said, scraping the rust off the climbing frame with my toe. There were cones and red tape around our usual corner. Two workmen were high up on a hydraulic platform, fixing new lights to the top of a pole. "Dad's working, so I guess we'll stay at home."

"Maybe I could come over and we could write stories?" said Izzy.

"Yeah, maybe," I said.

We watched as the platform sank down to the ground and the two men jumped off. One of the men took a key out of the control panel and threw it to the other. "Are they taking this away tonight?"

"Nah," said his mate. "Spoke to the boss. She said they'll be along for it tomorrow."

They gathered up their tools, scraggy bits of packaging

tape and empty boxes. With a last look up at the new lights, they headed off across the playground.

"Cheerio, girls," they said as they passed. A slip of paper fluttered out of one of the boxes they were carrying. I ran across and fetched it.

DESPATCH NOTE: 1 x FF LIGHTING UNIT
(PLAY PARK)

That didn't mean much to me.

At the bottom of the slip was the name of the company. I took it across to Izzy.

"STATE SECURITY AND – " I read. "What's that word, Izzy?

She looked across. "Surveillance."

"STATE SECURITY AND SURVEILLANCE SERVICES. What does surveillance mean?"

"Not sure," said Izzy. "Something to do with surveys, I guess."

"Maybe," I said. "Though they didn't ask *us* any questions."

"Izzy! Home time!" Izzy's mum was waving from across the playground. Izzy swung her bags over her shoulder and set off. "I'll see you when I get back!" she shouted.

"See ya," I said, but I wasn't concentrating. Because the other thing on the paper slip, next to the company name, was a big red spot.

Eventually Shannon told us it was time for us to go too. Back in the lounge, I pulled out the padded, heavy brown envelope that Mrs Scott had given each of us at home time. The contents spilled all over the carpet: ten smaller envelopes and boxes, each with a large coloured number on the outside. Also in the big envelope was a sheet of paper. There wasn't much on it: just the words *Play Pack* surrounded by trees, and a parrot on a swing. Underneath it said:

INSTRUCTIONS FOR USE

1. OPEN THE FIRST PACK.
LET THE WORLD KNOW YOU LIVE IN A PLAY HOUSE!

2. OPEN THE OTHER PACKS: IN ANY ORDER, ON ANY DAY. HAVE FUN!

3. RUN OUT OF PACKS? FIND YOUR FRIENDS AND GET CREATIVE!

I'm not massively keen on people telling me what to do, so I didn't follow the instructions. I opened pack 10 first, a little white carton. Inside there was a pack of playing cards, and a little booklet: *Card games for kids*. Nice. I had no idea how to play card games, but nice, even so.

Pack number 6 was a colouring book.

Pack number 8 was a pack of Plasticine.

Pack number 4 was some street chalk.

(Can you tell I like even numbers?)

Pack number 2 was a book: *Little Fells for Little Fellas*

55

(and girls). What a terrible title.

I turned to the odd numbers. Inside numbers 3,5,7 and 9 I found a packet of magnets, shadow puppet instructions, a cookbook and a nature spotter handbook.

The front door banged open: Dad was back. He didn't seem surprised to see all the mess on the floor, but then the floor was often messy.

"Wotcha," he said, blowing me a kiss from the doorway.

"Look at my Play Pack," I said. "We got it at school."

"Brilliant!" said Dad. "I'll grab a quick shower and then let's decorate the front door." Say what you like about Dad, he's always ready to play.

I frowned. Finally I opened pack number 1. Inside were a bunch of large, coloured foam letters with sticky pads on the back. And with the letters was a card.

This is my ____ _____
Unscramble the letters to complete the sentence and make a BIG statement to decorate your front door!'

Well it wasn't very hard: they'd told us the answer in the instructions. I arranged the letters: P-L-A-Y-H-O-U-S-E.

But the bigger question was this: how did Dad know we had to decorate the door?

Reggie came in, clutching his Number 1 pack. "We need to – "

"– decorate the front door, yes I know," I said. "I got one too."

"Dad!" Shannon was shouting from her bedroom.

"Can we do it now?" Reggie asked me.

"DAD!"

"In a minute, Reggie. Just waiting for Dad to finish his shower." I could hear the water running.

"DAD!" Shannon was shrieking now.

From the bathroom, a muffled shout. "Stop *yelling*, Shannon. What is it?"

"The internet's stopped working," she yelled back.

"I'm going to do my letters down in a line," said Reggie.

"I said the internet's not working!"

"I'm. Having. A. Shower!" bellowed Dad.

"Aargh!" screamed Shannon in frustration, and slammed her bedroom door so hard the front door rattled.

And that's how our Happy Easter began.

Chapter 9
BACK HILL

THE INTERNET WAS still off an hour later.

Shannon didn't stop complaining. "This is so *annoying!* I've used up, like, half my data already."

"You'll live," said Dad, opening a jumbo pack of The Chicken Stir Fry You Actually Cook in the Oven.

"Have you checked the router?"

"It's nothing to do with that," said Dad, tipping the contents all over a baking tray. It looked like frozen sick. "It was on the radio, they're doing something with the exchange at the bottom of the valley."

"When's it going to be fixed?"

"What do I look like, a telecom engineer?" Dad slammed the oven door. "I don't know, they said it could be a week or two."

"A WEEK? You are joking, right?" Shannon was sticking her chin out now. Reggie and I were sat at the table, trying to arrange our Play Pack letters into rude words. We looked at each other, because we knew what was coming.

Dad turned to face Shannon. "Relax, love. There's nothing you can do about it, and it isn't the end of the world. You could always, I dunno, put your phone down."

"That's easy for you to say," said Shannon. "You

haven't got any friends. You seriously don't understand."

"Here we go," I muttered. Reggie put his hands over his ears and screwed his eyes up tight.

Dad shrugged his shoulders and turned his palms outwards – just like Melissa had done the day before.

Shannon grabbed handfuls of her own hair and screamed. A proper, scare-the-ghosts-away scream. And then she turned on one heel and marched out – slamming the door, of course.

Dad was facing away from us, grabbing the edge of the counter with white-knuckled fingers. I could hear him breathing hard.

Finally, he spoke. "Never mind her. Let's focus on the things that matter. Will this be enough for you, or do you want some of these new Springy Thingy fries to go with it?"

I'm guessing Dad hadn't got the note about healthy eating.

Shannon didn't come down for tea.

"Dad, how did you know about the letters?" I asked.

Dad looked at me, puzzled.

"In the Play Pack? The ones for the front door?"

"Oh those. They told us you'd be getting them at that school meeting. Is there any good stuff in there?"

"Not bad," I said. "The chalks are good, and the Plasticine."

"And the magnets are cool," added Reggie.

"We'll have to give them a go over the holidays," said

Dad. "Right, let's stick these letters up, shall we?"

And so we stuck the coloured PLAY HOUSE foam letters on the front door: mine went horizontally, and Reggie's spelled the same words out vertically, starting from the first "P".

That left us with a "P" spare.

"Can I have a pee please Dad?"

"You've left your pee on the floor, Thora."

I stuck it on Reggie. "There's pee on your back!"

When we couldn't think of any more pee jokes we went in for a game of *Race Max 2*, which works OK even without the internet.

"Are you working tomorrow, Dad?" I asked.

"No, I'm off. Melissa's coming round in the morning. I thought we might climb up Back Hill if it's nice, maybe take the kite. Fancy that?"

"Yeah!" shouted Reggie. "We haven't done that for ages."

"Great," said Dad. "I'm sure she'll will be up for it, I'll text her tonight."

"She'll probably run up and wait for us at the top," I said.

It looked like I might be right, too; when Melissa let herself in after breakfast the next morning she was already in her stretchy running tights and a red t-shirt. Her dark glossy hair was tied back with a rainbow hair band, and her blue-green eyes were sparkling.

"Hey kids!" she said, dropping her bag in the hall and

breezing into the kitchen to give Dad a kiss. "It's awesome out there. Are we ready to hit the hills?"

"Just need my trainers," I said, finding them under the sofa. As I laced them up, HOUSE 2.0 caught my eye: the living room window was no longer pencil, but a thick, confident ink line.

"I've got the kite!" yelled Reggie, grabbing it from the kitchen table and running out of the door.

"Right, reckon we're all set," said Dad as I rejoined him in the hall. "Shannon, you ready to roll?" he shouted up the stairs.

Melissa raised her eyebrows. "A full house, eh? Impressive."

Dad smiled. "She's run out of data on her phone. Says she might as well come because there's nothing else to do."

"Oi, I heard that," said Shannon, gallumphing down the stairs. "I thought I'd hang out with you losers instead."

"We're truly honoured by your presence," said Dad, bowing low as he gestured everyone out of the door. Shannon slapped him on his bald spot as she passed and Dad tried to kick her up the bum in return, but nearly fell over instead.

"Hey Thora, switch the radio off will you. And grab me a can of pop from the fridge while you're at it, I need all the energy I can get."

I ducked back inside and rooted around in the fridge, looking for Dad's Coke, half-listening to the news on the radio.

"So that was child psychologist and chief architect of the Prime Minister's "Healthy Life" initiative, Dr Geoff Wharton. So let's turn our attention to that village in the North West he was

61

talking about, where this new radical agenda is being played out before the eyes of the nation. Jack Smith has the last broadcast before the self-imposed media blackout begins. You're outside the village, Jack, what can you tell us?"

"Thora! Thora! Are you coming?"

"Yeah, hang on, Dad," I said, finding the Coke at last underneath a bag of courgettes.

"Thanks, Jim. This sleepy village, its 200 children and their parents are about to embark on an unusual – some would say bizarre – social experiment that is likely to make or break this new Prime Minister's fortunes. The ground rules were set yesterday at a special assembly when –"

"Thora! We're all waiting for you!"

I ran across and flicked the switch. Politics on the radio. I doubt there is anything more boring in the world.

The five of us argued, elbowed and joked our way to the church in the bright sunshine before skirting the graveyard and setting off up the zigzag path up Back Hill. The insults soon dried up, replaced by heavy breathing and the scrunch of feet on stones. Reggie ran out in front, with me some way behind. Melissa and Dad followed, talking quietly, while Shannon was at the back – taking her own sweet time as usual.

I caught up with Reggie at the bench. From there the village looked like something out of Postman Pat: a jumble of model houses and crumpled tissue paper trees. Toy cars beetled up the windy road from the distant town where wisps of cotton wool rose from the factory chimney.

Back in the village I could see three bright yellow toy diggers in the play park, two miniature tipper trucks, and a dozen Plasticine men with spades and white helmets. I wondered what they were doing.

"Which one is our house?" asked Reggie, for the hundredth time.

I pointed to the curve of the cul-de-sac and our house, which sat mid-way down the straight bit. "It's easy," I said. "Look for the one next to the messy garden." Our garden looked immaculate from there – but only because Enid's old house next door was a jungle.

Dad puffed up to join us, with Melissa trotting along beside him.

"Abs, hamstrings, gluteals, calf muscles," Melissa was saying to Dad. "They're all getting a work-out. You'll feel it tomorrow."

"Never mind that, I'm feeling it today," said Dad. "Shove up, I need to sit down."

"Nice of you to save me a seat," said Shannon as she strolled up. She plopped herself on top of Dad, who made a muffled "oof!" noise.

He elbowed Shannon to one side so he could breathe, and for a moment none of us spoke.

"We came up here in the snow once," he said. "Do you remember, Shannon?"

Shannon shook her head, swinging her hair into Dad's face. He blew it clear.

"You weren't very old. But you, me and Rosie got all our gear on and you made it all the way to the top, even though the snow came up to your knees. I tried to help, but you were determined to do it on your own."

Dad waved the arm that wasn't trapped under Shannon out across the valley. "It was astonishing. You could hardly see the village under the snow. Phone lines went down. Everything came to a stop, it was like we were the only village in the world. Completely cut off, we were."

It was hard to imagine that now. Flashes of vibrant spring green dotted the village, a slight heat haze already softening the view. Only a small section of the fell opposite was still in shade, and sunlight glinted on the fence that ran alongside the cart track up to the head of the valley. A kestrel hovered above the houses, level with our bench, its wings fluttering in the slight breeze.

"Only one tractor made it through the snow on the first day to rescue us, and even then it couldn't get back down again. I couldn't get to work. And the school boiler broke down, so you and Rosie had a week off."

"That is so lucky," said Reggie. "A whole week to play."

"We went sledging in those fields over there. We made snowmen in the garden at the vicarage, until the grumpy old vicar told us off. And I broke one of the school windows in a snowball fight. Rosie killed me for that, said she'd have to tell the headmaster when she got back to work."

"Then what happened?" I asked.

"The snow started to melt, and everyone got fed up of having wet trousers," said Dad. "And then they ran out of milk at the shop, and nobody was very happy about that."

Dad shoved Shannon off his lap. "But it was fun while it lasted. You wouldn't get that happening now."

"Oh I don't know," said Melissa. "Never say never. Right, come on you lazy bones. Last one to the top has to carry the kite back down."

Chapter 10
SHANNON

THE MYSTERY OF the diggers that we'd seen from the bench on Back Hill was soon solved. For the whole of that first week of the holidays we watched as workmen installed a brand new play park. Shannon was supposed to be looking after us but she spent most of the time sitting at the other end of the park with her mates.

The rusty old swings and roundabout were gone on the first day, loaded by crane onto a truck that growled out of the village. Two days of earth-moving followed, swallowing up flowerbeds to create a much larger, open space. By the fourth day we were bringing sandwiches and crisps down so we didn't miss a thing and it was worth it, because the new equipment started to arrive.

First to be installed was a huge witch's hat – a cone of ropes and bars that rotated, reaching high into the air. A wooden fort was assembled around the outside featuring control towers, rope swings, twisty tube slides, a climbing wall and a zipwire that swooped down from the highest point.

By the end of the week there were new swings, a giant glockenspiel, balance beams and a full set of outdoor gym equipment for grown-ups.

The final installation was a massive bike rack. I'd never seen anything quite like it: there were different sized spaces for different sized bikes, and each one had a small touchscreen, although these were switched off.

One, two, three, four... I counted the spaces under my breath. "That's a bit stupid," I said to Izzy. "Thirty spaces, and hardly any of us have got bikes."

"Maybe they didn't know what else to put in the space," said Izzy.

"Maybe." I licked my finger to get the last of the cheesy bits from the bottom of my crisp packet. "I wonder when we'll be able to have a go on the fort."

As I was saying this, one of the workmen was passing by. "Should be all done by Saturday, love," he said. He stopped and looked back. "That's the best play park for fifty miles, that is." He reached a finger under his hat to scratch his head. "Still can't understand why we're putting it in this tiny village, but... "

"Saturday!" I whispered to Izzy as he walked off.

"That's only... what day is it today?"

"Thursday," said Izzy.

I counted. "Only two days to go!"

"Exciting, isn't it," said Melissa when I told her at breakfast. She had been staying with us the whole week, and only disappeared for short periods during the day while Dad was at work. The rest of the time she sat on Dad's bed with her laptop, occasionally shutting the door to make a phone call.

"Waste of money," said Shannon. She was sitting at the kitchen table, spinning her phone on the table. "They should spend it getting the internet fixed."

Melissa ignored her.

"I think it will be brilliant," said Reggie. "I can't wait. Charlie says he's going to get up at 5 o'clock to make sure he's the first person on the zipwire."

"Hmm. I'm not sure what Charlie's mum will think about that," said Melissa.

"What does *surveillance* mean?" I asked.

Melissa paused. "Why do you ask that, love?"

"I just saw it somewhere."

"Well, it means –"

"Spying," interrupted Shannon. "Like they're doing on us."

"It depends on the context," said Melissa. "It doesn't have to be James Bond stuff. In some cases, it means that someone is looking after you, without necessarily being there in the room."

Shannon snorted.

"So in the play park..."

"That play park is about as good as they get," said Melissa. "The guys who are installing it really know what they're doing. And it'll give you guys something productive to do during the day, which is great." She looked at Shannon.

"I don't know why you're looking at me," snapped Shannon. "There's no way I'm going to some stupid playground."

Melissa dropped a tray onto the worktop with a clatter and turned to face Shannon. "So what *are* you going to do for the next week? Sit on a bench with your friends looking miserable, complaining about how Daddy hasn't given you any more data? How about knuckling down and getting some study done?"

It was Shannon's turn to ignore Melissa. She picked at a hole in the table cloth with her chewed fingernail.

"You're nearly eighteen," continued Melissa. "By your age I'd got a job and was saving for my first car. No clothes allowance, no hand outs, no selfies, and definitely no mobile phone."

"That was, like, 50 years ago," Shannon retorted. "Things are different now. Stuff like *this* matters," she said, brandishing her mobile phone. "You just don't understand."

The cutlery clinked as Melissa emptied the dishwasher. Reggie's chair scraped as he got up and walked round to my side.

Melissa paused, saucepan in hand. "I know more than you give me credit for, young lady. And if I were you, I'd – "

"Well I'm not you, am I," hissed Shannon at Melissa's back. "You're not my mum, you're just Dad's girlfriend. We all know you'll be gone as soon as you finish your work. You're a visitor."

Clink, clack, ting. Melissa carried on emptying the dishwasher.

Shannon was livid, but she wasn't finished. "And I can't see many jobs going round here, unless you want me to join the other losers stacking frozen pizzas at the factory?" She tapped the side of her head. "Don't you see? You don't get to tell me what I can do."

A rustling noise made us all look round. Dad was standing at the door, carrier bag in hand.

"But I do," he said softly. "Those 'losers' at the factory, as you call them, are supporting their families. They're helping our company. And our company makes your food. The money they pay me buys your clothes and your bus tickets and your hot showers and your school trips. It even pays for your precious data."

Dad walked in. He ran his hand through my hair and then Reggie's before plucking Shannon's phone off the table.

"Give that back!" Shannon shouted.

"You don't need it. They told us today the internet will be down for quite a while. And since you won't be getting more credit any time soon, there's no point in a phone, is there?"

"Sorry guys," Dad said, turning to us. "Time for a clean break, otherwise it's not fair on Shannon. No iPad or consoles either." I guessed that meant another *Race Max 2* evening was out of the question.

"Un-be-lievable," said Shannon, getting to her feet. "You can't even see what *that woman* is doing to this family, can you?" She spat the words out, her face screwed up with anger.

Melissa watched as Dad walked up to Shannon. Reggie was leaning into me; I felt a shudder pass through him. Shannon stood firm with her hands on her hips; she glared up at Dad, breathing hard through flared nostrils.

Dad raised his hands. I felt Reggie flinch, and saw Shannon recoil slightly. But Dad reached out and held her shoulders.

"It's early days, Shannon," he said, quietly. Shannon twisted, but he held her firm. "You're feeling trapped, and I get that. Your mum was the same. But you won't be in this house for ever. And when you head out into the world, *then* you'll find a battle that's worth the fight. For now, you're practising. And when you come back, if you come back, I'll always be here for you."

Dad released Shannon, and she paused. She took a breath to answer back, but changed her mind. She turned and left the room, leaving the door open behind her.

Chapter 11
MYSTERY AT THE
PLAY PARK

IF THEY GAVE out awards for days of the week, surely Saturday would win. The start of the weekend. Six days left to do homework. Everyone out playing while mums and dads do their jobs. Perfect.

This particular Saturday was Day of the Decade though, because as the workman predicted, the new play park was open. Reggie and I gobbled down our breakfast in front of the telly and HOUSE 2.0 (now featuring a new upstairs window: something new was being added every week now). The first thing we saw when we arrived was Charlie whizzing down the zipwire. Dad once described Charlie as a solid little unit, like a remote-controlled battering ram. He was hanging on sideways, crazy hair waving everywhere, screaming in delight. As he came to a stop his head bonked along the new rubber matting, but he didn't even seem to notice.

"It's BRILLIANT!" he shouted at us, crumpling to the ground.

I didn't need telling: I ran for the climbing wall and hoiked my way up the coloured handholds to the top of the fort, right up high near the new lights. I wasn't surprised to see that they looked like giant versions of the grey satsumas that had been installed at home.

For a moment I was on my own, but it wasn't going to last: from my lookout I could see out across the village. And in every direction I could see kids running towards the play park. A few younger ones were with parents, but many of them were on their own. Within minutes the park was a blur of tipping, spinning and sliding, with queues forming for the most popular equipment.

"Hey Thora!"

Reggie and Charlie had climbed right to the very tip of the Witch's Hat. They were clutching on to each other, swaying precariously like pirates up a mast. Charlie let go to wave at me and nearly fell off – Reggie grabbed him just in time.

"This is BRILLIANT!" Charlie shouted again.

First to join me at the top of the fort was Izzy.

"So I found out what it means," I told her.

"What?"

"Surveillance."

Izzy looked blank.

"You know, on the piece of paper from the workmen."

"Oh, that."

"It means they're watching us."

"Who are?

"I don't know."

"Why would they do that?"

I don't know that either," I admitted.

Izzy shrugged. It wasn't much of a discovery, I had to admit.

"What happened to Code Club?" I asked. Code Club is where you write programs on computers to make them do stuff, like draw patterns on the floor or make buzzers go off. Lots of the kids in the top years go. Izzy's dad, who works on computers, helps to organise it at Shannon's school, so they drive down the valley every Saturday.

"Oh, it was cancelled," said Izzy. "Mr Rossi said the council wouldn't pay any more, and anyway it wasn't worth bothering because everyone would be here instead."

Mr Rossi was right. Equipment rippled with movement and colour as children hung off every bar and platform, hollering and shrieking. Others had joined us at the top of the fort, jostling to get a position where they could wave to their friends. There were children here I didn't even recognise; they must surely have travelled up from town.

Around the edges of the play park, sitting on benches or standing at the bars like daytrippers at the zoo, were small clutches of parents laughing and chatting. I could see Melissa; she spotted me and smiled.

"Race you to the bottom," said Izzy, and we climbed across the rope bridge, through tunnels and down slides like a real-life game of Snakes and Ladders. There we found Ailsa, perhaps the bossiest girl in our year, who was organising everyone into teams.

Izzy, Charlie and Reggie ran towards her: I ran the other way. I knew what would happen if I joined in: it would all be fine, and then it would be my turn to lead and everyone would turn to me for instructions. And then we'd lose, and they'd hate me. Better to watch. Nobody can blame you for that.

They chased each other in and out of the fort for

ages, tagging and taking prisoner, hiding and surprising. Charlie, Reggie and Izzy screamed past sometimes, not even noticing me. I couldn't wait until it was just the four of us again.

Over the other side of the park I spotted Shannon with her mates Alice and Tara. With their legs hooked over the monkey bars they swung gently upside down, like a new species of long-haired bat. They chatted away as if the rest of the world was upside down, and they were the right way up.

Finally, after a particularly hectic game of Capture the Castle, the others joined me on the astroturf bank, exhausted.

"We lost," groaned Izzy.

I was glad I hadn't joined in.

"I'm not going back to school," said Reggie, propping himself up on one elbow. "I'm going to play here, for ever."

"Yeah, for ever," said Charlie. "With no mums and dads."

"What would you eat, stupid?" asked Izzy.

I looked at Izzy and frowned. Charlie definitely isn't 'top set material', as the teachers say when they think we're not listening, but that was rude. Mind you, Charlie didn't seem to notice, or mind.

"We'd get pizzas delivered. Big piles of them," said Charlie.

"And then after we'd eaten them, we'd burn the boxes to keep warm," added Reggie.

"And how would you order the pizzas then, smarty pants?"

"On Charlie's tablet," said Reggie. "There's a pizza app, I saw it on the telly, it's easy."

"Nah, we'd have to shout for mum," said Charlie. "I don't have my tablet any more."

"What?" said Reggie, sitting up.

"Yeah, Dad took it away. Since the internet's not working, he said there's no point having it."

"That's exactly what my Dad said to Shannon," I said. There was a moment's silence.

"Doesn't it seem a bit weird to you? Everyone gets their iPads taken away after that weird assembly by Mr Wharton?"

"But hang on," said Izzy. "You didn't even have the internet on your tablet. So you couldn't have ordered pizzas anyway."

"Oh yeah, you're right." Charlie scratched his head. "I hadn't thought of that."

I sighed.

"Anyway," said Charlie, "he says I can have it back when the internet comes on again."

"*If* it comes on again." I looked around us. "Look at the mums and dads over there. Notice anything different?"

"Umm," said Izzy. "There's a lot of them, that's for sure."

"Something else," I said. "There's something missing."
The others shrugged.

"Phones," I said. "Nobody has got their phone." Not a single parent was rummaging in a bag or a pocket. Instead of the tops of their heads we could see faces chatting, smiling, or simply watching. No eyes-down. No jostling to get the best photo, no tip-tap status updating, no swiping.

"Why not? Where have they put them?" asked Reggie.

"I don't know, but it's not... normal."

The others looked for a moment longer, and carried on chatting about pizzas. But I watched the parents watching us. And I noticed the way that more cars than usual passed by, each one slowing for a look at the new play park, and at the children playing.

I couldn't shake the feeling that the grown-ups had put away their phones so that they could get a better look at us. And all this attention was starting to make me feel very uneasy.

Chapter 12
VILLAGE ASSEMBLY

WE PLAYED ON, but the situation was starting to become ridiculous as more and more parents turned up to watch. I spotted some of the class teachers and even Sheila, the lollipop lady: no uniform today, but she gave me a grin and a thumbs up.

Dad arrived and stood with Melissa.

"What're you doing here, Dad?" I asked.

"Bunked off work a bit early. I wanted to check out your new gear," he said. He glanced up at the church clock. "Go on then, show us what you can do."

As I ran back to the fort a reflection caught my attention. I shielded my eyes to look. Sandwiched between Charlie's mum and a granny were a couple, both dressed in black jogging bottoms and red t-shirts. I didn't recognise either of them, and their suntan suggested they definitely weren't from round here. The glint came from a large camera being carried by the man on his shoulder.

The woman saw me looking, and beckoned me with a pearly-white grin. She nudged her companion, and they stepped forward out of the crowd.

"Hi there," she said, bending down towards me, even though she was about the same height. "What's your name?"

"Thora," I said. "Thora Batty. Who are you?"

"Me and my friends are from the council." She pronounced "council" as if it were two separate words: coun-*sill*. "We're making a film about your fantastic new play park. Can I ask you a few questions?"

I looked at the round, blank lens. "I won't be on the telly, will I?"

She looked at the man, who shook his head slightly. "It's for staff, really, but we'd like to find out what you think. It'll be fun!" Before I could have chance to think she reached out, and swivelled me round slightly to face the man and his camera. "Ready? Just ignore the camera, and talk to me."

She put her arm around my shoulder. A red light came on and we waited. After a minute the man, who was wearing an earpiece, held up his fingers and counted down: "Three, two..." He mouthed the word one, and then made an OK sign with his free hand.

In an instant, the woman's expression changed completely: her eyes opened wider, her eyebrows went up, and she smiled as she talked – a clown's face with less make-up.

"Hey, it's Kristi here! And on this very special morning I'm here with one of the new users of the pilot play area, Thora Catty, and she's *very* excited, I have to tell you. So let's find out – "

"Batty," I said.

"Sorry?"

"Thora Batty. Not Catty." I might not have the most sensible name in the world – my mum called me that because she said I was wrinkly when I was born, like an old lady off the telly. But it drives me bananas when someone gets it wrong. It's not hard to remember.

"Ah yes, Thora Batty, I'm sorry," said Kristi, not looking sorry at all. She moved round to stand beside the cameraman. "So what do you think of your new play park?"

"It's great," I said, because it was. "The best one I've ever been to."

"What's your favourite thing about it?"

"Probably the fort," I said. "What's that big bike rack for, though?"

"So do you think you'll be using it a lot now?" said Kristi, ignoring my question.

"Yes, I guess so." I maybe sounded a bit dopey because I wasn't really concentrating. Over Kristi's shoulder I could now see two more teams of cameramen dressed in red and black, filming the children on the play equipment.

"Well it sounds like the fun has only just begun down here," she said to the camera. "We'll be covering all the action throughout the day with lots more coming up. But for now, it's back to you."

The camera's red light turned off, and Kristi's face returned to normal. "Thanks kiddo, off you go."

"What *is* the bike rack for though?" I asked. "It's not like many of us have even got bikes."

For the first time, Kristi met my gaze. "I promise, you'll find out soon enough, sweetie." She winked at me and then moved off with the cameraman towards the Witch's Hat.

"I've been on TV!" Izzy shouted to me.

"I haven't," I replied, from the top of a ladder. "Or at least I don't think so. What did they ask you?"

"Oh, nothing much, just if we were having fun. Stuff like that."

At the far end of the park, through the vehicle gates, a gigantic white truck was slowly reversing. With grunts and beeps it crawled towards us, guided by a team in red t-shirts.

As the front of the truck cleared the gateposts, a small group of adults followed on foot. I didn't recognise everyone but one immediate spot was Mr Frost, our head teacher, chatting to Mr Wharton. What on earth were they doing here?

The reversing truck slowed to a halt. The engine was switched off and the rear doors opened, though hanging rubber strips stopped us seeing what was inside.

By now all the children had stopped playing and the grown-ups were watching, too. I noticed that the camera crews were now filming the truck.

Onto the tailgate jumped Mr Frost and Mr Wharton. With a whine, the tailgate rose into the air. I scanned the side of the truck, looking for something I was sure I'd find: yep, there it was. A red spot, low down near the wheel.

"Ladies and gentlemen!"

Mr Frost isn't a quiet man at the best of times. And as children and grown-ups hushed, his voice – amplified by speakers somewhere in the truck – bounced back from the fells around.

"Ladies and gentlemen, children and parents of Rain & Shine Academy, and esteemed visitors, we are thrilled so

80

many of you could come today.

"Children, it looks as if you're making the most of our fabulous new play park. But we have one more surprise for you, and indeed for everyone in this lovely village." He paused for effect, grinning like he does in assembly.

"Now all we need is a volunteer, and *everything* will be revealed."

There was a burst of shouting and waving arms, as children everywhere tried to catch Mr Frost's attention. He consulted with Mr Wharton, before raising his hands for quiet. Gradually the yelling stopped, with just the occasional grunt from an over-enthusiastic waver.

"We need someone very responsible for this job," said Mr Frost in mock seriousness. "A proper ambassador for our village. So let's give a big hand to... Thora Batty!"

Me? A boulder landed with a thud in the pit of my stomach. I didn't even have my hand up! Everyone was clapping, shouting my name. Dad grinned, and gestured towards the truck; Izzy gave me a little push forward. And so to the sound of cheers and whoops, I walked across.

As I arrived, one of the men in red t-shirts greeted me. "Let's get you where everyone can see you," he said, and lifted me up by the armpits onto the platform.

My knees almost buckled at the sight. Hundreds of parents and children gazed up at me expectantly, waiting for me to embarrass myself somehow.

"Now then, follow Mr Frost's lead and don't do anything idiotic in front of your Mum and Dad," said Mr Wharton softly, so that nobody could hear. His breath smelled of stale coffee.

I looked up at him and blinked hard.

"I don't have a Mum. My Mum's dead." Normally I try to make it easier on people when they make that mistake. But not this time.

"Well, yes, of course," he blustered, the smile slipping for a moment. "But, aahm, you wouldn't want to look a fool in front of your friends either, would you –"

"Yes, thanks Geoff, maybe I'll take it from here," said Mr Frost. Mr Frost turned to the audience and put on his assembly voice.

"So I hear from one of our helpers that Thora here has noticed that our new play park isn't *quite* finished," Mr Frost said, smiling out at the crowd. "And that's because no play is complete without a ride on your bike, am I right, grown-ups?" A cheer went up from the adults, even Dad.

"So to make sure that everyone can get out and about around our village, our sponsors have come up with a *wheely* good idea. Wheely good. Wheely. Get it?" The crowd groaned, and Mr Frost took a little bow. "Thora, head on back into the truck and see what you can find."

He parted the flaps and I was happy to head back out of sight.

The truck was lit by lines of LED lights. A strong tang of metal and oil hung in the air. As my eyes adjusted I saw racks that stretched from floor to ceiling, and as far back as I could see. Stacked up, in row after gleaming row, were hundreds of shiny new red mountain bikes.

I grabbed the handlebars of the nearest bike and tugged, and with a clunk it rolled free. Taking a deep breath I pushed it out into the sunshine and stood squinting, feeling rather silly.

"Here she is, our first village spokesman," said Mr

Frost. "Spokesman, spokesman, geddit?" The crowd groaned again. "So children, Thora's holding the first of our fantastic Village Bikes. That's one of dozens we have back there in the truck for children and grown-ups too. From now on, wherever you live and wherever you want to go, grab one and pedal on your way. So no more excuses if you're late for school!"

While he was talking, Mr Wharton pressed a button and lowered the tailgate to the floor.

"So let's give Thora a big round of applause as she takes a spin over to the racks, and shows everyone how easy it is!"

I looked at Mr Frost, who tilted his head in encouragement.

"Do I need a helmet?" I whispered.

He covered the microphone on his lapel. "You'll be fine," he said. "Just don't fall off in front of the cameras."

I hadn't even thought of that, but now that was all I could think about. The saddle was about the right height, so off I pedalled.

"Bring on the revolution!" yelled Mr Frost as I wobbled my way across the play park to the bike rack.

A man guided me towards the end with the smaller docking stations. "Well done, honey! Now push it in."

As I slotted the front wheel home a rush of relief almost swamped me. I grabbed hold of the bike saddle for support as everything went blurry for a second. The docking screen switched on with a beep, and the world swam back into focus. Cartoon monkeys swung through trees and a parrot appeared. "You've cycled 87 metres and used 23 calories," she squawked in an American accent that was half bird, half computer. "Place your hand on the screen to add it to your account."

An outline of a hand appeared on the screen and I matched up my fingers.

"Well done, Thora!" squawked the parrot, who obviously knew more about me than I did about her. "Goodbye, and have a fun day!'

Chapter 13
WHAT DO YOU THINK, THORA?

THAT SECOND WEEK of the holidays was crazy. The village was jam-packed. Vans with satellite dishes carved up the grass verges. Reporters stood on our little village roundabout and filmed anything that moved, asking children to cycle around them 'just one more time'. Izzy and I spotted camera crews from the Netherlands, Norway, Sweden, Italy, Germany, America and Brazil.

Everywhere you went you could hear squawking parrots as we were asked to show the visitors how we check in and out at the racks. These had been installed in six places around the village and Shannon also spotted one from the school bus, installed on the edge of town.

"That's for masochists only," Dad told us. "Set off up that valley on a bike and it'll be the last ride you do."

More often than not the TV presenters would talk to other people and then ask if they knew where they could find "that Batty girl." And find me they did: at the play park, the library, or even knocking on our front door.

Then they'd pepper me with questions, and get my name wrong. I got called Thora Catty, of course, but also

Ratty, Tatty and even Fatty.

Reggie found it hilarious. He made faces at me from behind the camera to try and make me laugh, and asked me for my autograph. But for me it was anything but funny. Adults crowding round, inquiring faces up too close, wanting to know what I thought, how I felt, what my hopes and fears were for the future. I'd been here before: I didn't like it before, and I still didn't like it.

After one man got particularly close with his camera I ran upstairs, tears streaming down my face. Dad found me and called a halt to the doorstep circus, sending the disappointed crews away.

Shannon stayed at home, out of the limelight. Her only comment was that she could have made a fortune out of this if she'd been able to live stream it. It's safe to say she wasn't a big fan of the bikes, unless they took her straight to a nearby TV.

As the last TV vans coasted off down the valley the sound of diesel engines and generators was replaced with ticking spokes, the *brrring!* of bike bells and the occasional cry of "Watch out, here I come!"

It took a little while for everyone to get the hang of the docks. You had to touch the screen before the bike was released, and then again when you returned it. That added the energy you'd used to your account and you could tap the screens to see leaderboards for everyone in your age range, in your street and even in your family.

We found out what happened if you forgot to return

the bike when Charlie left one by the Witch's Hat. The bike emitted a loud chirping noise followed by a robotic American voice: "Bike immobile. Please return to dock."

Charlie looked down. "You're not the boss of me!" he shouted at it, grinning.

To our delight, the bike answered back. "Repeat: Bike immobile. Alerting the parents of CHARLIE. BARNES. In five minutes."

We'd never seen him scramble down the Witch's Hat so fast! He grabbed the talking bike and marched it back to the rack. Tapping in, he peered at the screen. "Hey, I've been docked 500 calories!" he moaned. We all laughed, but after that we made sure we always returned the bikes to the racks.

It wasn't just the children who used them: the grown-ups did, too. One Saturday morning while Shannon was still in bed – although that meant any time before lunch – Dad suggested the rest of us should go for a ride around the village.

This was about as likely as Shannon offering to play a game of hide and seek with us.

"What, you?" I said. "I don't think they come with stabilisers."

"Cheeky. Why shouldn't I join in the fun?"

"Well, because..."

"Because you're too fat!" shouted Reggie.

"Oi! There are pigs that would sell their mother for a potbelly like this. And besides, it doesn't stop me doing *this* though, does it?" said Dad, turning Reggie upside down. "Don't you worry about me, I was Kent Junior BMX champion back in the day. Once a pedal powerhouse, always a pedal powerhouse."

We touched in by the play park, setting off a chorus of robo greetings.

Reggie sped off, but I stuck around: if there were going to be embarrassing scenes I wanted to be there. But I was disappointed. Dad pushed off and after a few wobbles he was soon circling around and then we were off, the four of us looping around the village like we'd been cycle buddies for years.

"I'd forgotten how much fun this was," said Dad, thumping down off a kerb. "They're not bad little machines, these things." He leaned back and yanked on the handlebars; the front wheel lifted off the ground for a moment. "Bit heavy for my taste. Not much chance of popping a wheelie."

"It's not the bike that's heavy," called Melissa, wheeling alongside.

"Cheeky. You might be right, though," said Dad. "Maybe I should start cycling to work."

"You?" I said. "On that bike you won?"

"No, I'll take one of these," said Dad, standing up on the pedals. "How hard can it be? Then I can kick your butt on that energy chart thingy. I'll probably get a medal or they'll put a statue of me in on the village green."

"Oh John. You're like an six-year-old trapped in a 45-year-old's body," said Melissa, shaking her head.

"Shame it's the body of a pregnant mum," said Dad, patting his belly. "Still, only one way to sort that out. Race you to the shop!"

"Yeah but how come there's been nothing on *our* TV about it?" said Shannon. She was picking unhappily at the vegetables in the genuine stir fry that Melissa had made. But to be fair, so was everybody else. They didn't taste... real.

"Dunno," said Dad, pushing his definitely-not-empty plate forward. "I think I'm full. Thanks, love."

"All those TV crews, but there's nothing on our telly. Don't you think that's weird?"

Dad looked at Melissa. "Guess so. Help me out here, Melissa, any ideas?"

"Well," said Melissa, carefully spearing another carrot. "Maybe... you just missed it."

Everyone looked at Melissa in disbelief. Since her phone had been taken away, Shannon and the TV had become inseparable. She hadn't missed a thing.

"OK, maybe not. I guess there are already bike schemes in London and places like that, so it's not as interesting to people in this country."

Shannon looked up at the clock: nearly seven. "I'm going to check the news tonight," she said, and pushed her chair back.

"Shannon!" said Dad. "Put your plate in the dish – " but it was too late. She was gone.

But not for long.

"Dad! Dad!" she shouted from the lounge.

"Yes, my darling angel," said Dad, clearing the dishes.

"There's something wrong with the telly! What have you done with it?"

"I'll clear up here," said Melissa. "You go."

Dad pulled a face, and Reggie and I followed him

89

through to the lounge.

Shannon was lying in her usual spot: legs hanging over the end of the sofa, head propped up with a cushion. She was frowning as she stabbed away at the remote control. 'Channel unavailable' said a message on the screen.

"Look, nothing! All the channels have gone!" Just as she said that, the TV erupted with the theme tune for The One Show, and Matt Baker appeared.

"Looks OK to me," shouted Dad, motioning for Shannon to turn it down.

"No, but that's only BBC One. Look, all the satellite channels have gone," said Shannon, flicking through the big numbers.

"What about Nickelodeon?" I asked.

"Gone."

"CBBC?" said Reggie, hopefully.

"Gone. They've all gone. We've just got... " Shannon started at 1 again. "BBC One, BBC Two, ITV, Channel – whoah, even Channel 4 has gone! You've got to fix that, Dad."

"Hang on, why me?" said Dad. "And besides, I haven't touched anything. Must be a transmitter down, or something." Dad flopped down onto the sofa, and grabbed the remote. "Now budge over, I want Matt Baker to tell me why there aren't as many hedgehogs as there used to be, and maybe he'll show us some funny-shaped vegetables."

"Aargh! You're IMPOSSIBLE!" said Shannon, and flounced off to her bedroom.

"That did the trick," said Dad, turning the telly off. "I don't really want to watch that rubbish. Who wants to see if they can balance more Lego bricks on their belly than me?'

Chapter 14
BACK TO SCHOOL

YOU KNOW THOSE awards for Days of the Week I was talking about? When Saturday wins? Well everybody knows that Monday would come bottom. It's nobody's friend, except maybe Izzy's. Five days of school ahead. Boring whole school assembly. Literacy and maths until they're coming out of your ears.

And of all the Mondays, the one that would get the most boos would definitely be the one after the Easter holidays. It's months until the next holiday, the weather is still rubbish, and you haven't even got Christmas to look forward to.

There were a couple of changes, though. For starters, HOUSE 2.0 now had a downstairs window. "I'm saving a bit harder," said Dad when we asked him.

And then Dad said I could walk to school on my own, or with Reggie at least. "You're old enough," he said. "It'll be good practice for when you get the school bus." Shannon would be leaving the high school in town just as I'd be starting. "Unless you fancy cycling to school?" said Dad. "You could ride in with me."

To the relief of all our neighbours our unlovable car hadn't backfired its way off the drive for days. Instead

Dad had got up earlier – "so nobody can see me in cycling shorts" – slipped on a rucksack and borrowed a bike for the journey to work. The trip down the valley was easy, of course, but at the end of the first day he'd staggered through the door. "Water, water," he'd gasped, before collapsing on the kitchen floor, groaning. But he's even more determined than me, and that was the beginning: he'd been cycling ever since.

Shannon shook her head at me in warning. "Don't even think about it," she said through a mouthful of cornflakes. "I walked home once, it nearly killed me. It's like climbing Everest."

"What a wuss," said Dad. "Those Village Bikes have about 324 gears. And if you take the cart track on the way down there are some gnarly drop-offs I can show you." He stood up. "Right you two, get on your way. Bikes or no bikes, you don't want to upset that oddball headteacher of yours."

Reggie and I crossed the play park and continued out onto the main road. We reached the crossing before either of us noticed that Sheila wasn't there. Instead, a man and a woman in yellow hi-vis jackets stood in the middle of the road with their backs to us, chatting away. I recognised the man holding the lollipop instantly because his jacket only came half way down his back: Mr Wharton. They didn't see us.

"So do it like this," he was saying. "Make sure you hold the lollipop close to the children, otherwise it'll be a jolly big waste of time."

I had no idea that holding a lollipop was so difficult.

"And then as they cross, stay close behind them and

make sure you're not accidentally covering up these small holes in the handle – " Mr Wharton spotted us, and spun round.

"Oh goodness gracious, customers already! Good morning, children!"

I now recognised the woman: it was Kristi, the one from the council who had interviewed me. "Hi!" she said brightly. "Great to see you again!"

Weird to see *you* again, I thought.

"Rightio," said Mr Wharton, "I think you're all set here. I'll leave you to it. Cheery-bye!" He yanked off his yellow jacket and set off towards the school.

"Hey, Mr Wharton!" I shouted after him. He paused, and turned towards me. His eyes narrowed. "Yes?"

"Where has Sheila gone?"

"She... she's having her hip replaced. She went into hospital at the weekend, won't be out for a week or two. Bed-bound. I expect she'll be off work for a couple of months at least. Right, on you go, or you'll be late. Have fun!"

Reggie pulled my hand. "Come on," he urged. "I promised Charlie I'd help him with his homework."

Mr Wharton was some distance away now, but he appeared to be talking to himself while sticking his finger in his ear. Meanwhile Kristi was fiddling with her brand new lollipop, trying to arrange her fingers on the stick like it was a recorder, and walking so closely behind us as we crossed that she trod on my heel. There was something *very* odd about those two.

At school, all the talk was about the missing telly channels. The reception had never been great in our valley, mind you, but now all we could get was three channels. Even worse, the children's TV finished at 6 o'clock.

"It's not fair," said Izzy, as we stood around our bags. "*Elizabethan Engineering* was on last night, and I can't even watch it on catch-up. I was so bored I rubbed out all my maths homework and did it again."

Charlie gave Izzy a puzzled look and scratched his head. You could almost smell the burning as he tried to work out why anyone would do that. Eventually he smiled: he'd given up. "Have you finished yet, Reggie?"

Reggie was kneeling down, checking Charlie's homework. "Yeah. You've got two answers right. Plus your name, but I don't think that counts."

"Of course it does. Thanks, Reggie." He tucked his book back into his bag. "You can come round later, maybe watch *Nature's Bravest Squirrels* on our 3D TV." Charlie paused. He can't really think and do things at the same time. "Oh yeah. I forgot, it's on Channel 5."

Charlie shrugged, flicked Reggie on the ear and they both ran indoors, laughing.

Mr Frost's first assembly after the holiday was always a long one, and that day was no exception. I think the days off gave him time to think up lots more bad jokes, although I bet he didn't make Mrs Frost sit cross-legged until her legs went numb, listening to him rattle on.

He wandered across to the back of the stage. He'd

been doing this a lot in assembly recently, pacing back and forwards, throwing his arms around and delivering every message as if he was performing Shakespeare.

But this time he had a destination: the big school crest on the wall. This had been put up a couple of years before when the school had been taken over, apparently because it wasn't very good. Frosty had been parachuted in from a mega-school to sort us out. He didn't literally arrive by parachute, though I bet he would have enjoyed that. He made everyone buy a new uniform. He added on another couple of years so you stayed until you're 13, and the Government would give him more money. And he did a sponsorship deal with a local waterproofing company and renamed it *Rain & Shine Academy*. Our logo was a sun and a raincloud, naturally, but it was the motto which had got everyone talking: *Soak up knowledge, dazzle the world.* "Sounds like something I'd use to clean the toilet," Dad had muttered.

"This," said Mr Frost, waving his hand at the crest, "is why we all get up in the morning." Speak for yourself, I thought. "To drink in knowledge, and shine a little more every day."

Someone pretended to be sick near the back of the hall – it might have been a teacher – but Mr Frost ignored it.

"But to do our best learning, we must be in tip-top form. So let me ask you, Shiners, what can *we* do to help *you* be the very best person you can be?" Shiners is what he calls children at the school.

Frosty scanned the room. Nobody seemed keen to answer, perhaps because none of us understood the question.

"The answer is right in front of you, underneath our motto. *A healthy eating school.* That is what it says. That is what Mr Wharton spoke about so memorably last term."

All eyes turned to Mr Wharton who was standing, arms crossed, and who nodded slightly in acknowledgement.

"But are we grown-ups doing enough to help you to get your fruit and veg? Are we?"

This clearly wasn't a question that needed an answer either, and nobody tried. "Well let's ask the woman who knows... Let's give a big Rain & Shine Academy welcome to Mrs Scrincher and her fabulous team of chefs!"

The doors to the hall banged open and in trooped the famously miserable Mrs Scrincher, head of the school kitchen, and her seven helpers. But half-hearted claps turned to cheers as we saw that their stained, tatty aprons were gone. Instead, each adult wore a different vegetable outfit, as if they were going to a fancy dress party. Mrs Scrincher herself was in a bright red dress with a green cap – a tomato, I guessed, or maybe a strawberry. She was followed by a leek (that was Mrs Weatherly, who's tall and skinny), an aubergine, a carrot, an onion, a potato, a runner bean and finally Mrs Plumpton, dressed in a dirty white and purple outfit with a leafy green hat. "I'm a turnip," I saw her mouth to one of the confused teachers as she passed. All of them looked as miserable as sin.

"As you know, we have already introduced more vegetables to our menus," said Frosty. "But Mrs Scrincher reports that take-up has been somewhat... unenthusiastic, would that be right?" Mrs Scrincher nodded her head and her tufty green cap flapped in agreement.

"So from today, it's probably easier to talk about what

96

you *won't* be able to eat at lunchtime. I'm extremely proud to announce that from today, Rain & Shine will be the first Puddingless Academy in the country!"

Did I hear him right? We all looked at each other, looking for reassurance.

"That's right!" said Frosty above the mutterings of grumpy children. "They weren't doing you any good, so we've got rid of them entirely, which makes it possible to say that this is now a Sugar Free School!"

Mrs Scrincher smiled a measly, thin smile – perhaps because that meant she didn't have to make any puddings, but probably because we were all unhappy, and that always seemed to give her a lift.

"It gets better!" announced Mr Frost. It could hardly get any worse, I thought. He was on a roll now, bouncing around the stage, weaving in and out of the vegetable ladies. "There's no point in a healthy eating school if you children spend all your pocket money on sweets at Mrs Levett's shop, is there?"

Please don't say you're removing them there as well, I thought.

"So I'll be asking Mrs Levett to remove the sweets there as well!" Frosty was now having to shout above the grumbles, and even a few low boos.

"That's right, I can tell you're all impressed," he said, smiling. He stood back and grinned triumphantly. "But don't stop shopping, because I'll also be asking her to introduce a new range of fruit and veg snacks. And even better, your parents have agreed to help out, too – packed lunches will now contain only savoury foods."

Frosty looked around the room at the glum faces of

pupils and staff. "I can see you need a little time to take in all this good news, so let's all stand to sing the school anthem, *Sunshine on a Rainy Day.*'

Chapter 15
THE REFLECTION ROOM

AFTER WE'D FINISHED our ridiculous school song Mr Frost did his end of assembly announcements. He had quite a few. He started by giving house points to anyone who'd arrived at school using a Village Bike. He bounced around the stage, sometimes stepping down into the audience to shake someone's hand or ask them to come up and take a bow.

Then he told us they'd been very busy in the school during the holidays fitting new gym equipment. Some of that was hanging on the wall besides him, and he yanked down some bars and did a few pull-ups, huffing and puffing in his blue suit. The younger children thought this was brilliant, of course, and he lapped up the laughter.

And of course there was also the new bike rack, he told us. But that meant there wouldn't be any space for the PTA to run their after-school ice cream stall any more, which he was sure we would all agree was in fact a good thing. We didn't agree, but he didn't care.

"And there's one more change that all Shiners should know about," he said. "Where the computer room used to be, we now have a drop-in Reflection Room. You'll earn bonus house points every time you go in. So whatever you're feeling – "

Reggie's hand shot up. Nobody asks questions in assembly, but his class sits near the front, so Mr Frost couldn't really ignore him. "Yes, Reggie? I do hope this is breathtakingly important."

"What happened to the old room?" asked Reggie. "What will we do for computer club?"

"Well I don't know if you've noticed, but the internet has been cut off to our valley," he said, as if he were speaking to an idiot. "It's likely to be off until next year. And what use is a computer without the internet, I ask you?"

Next year! I could dig a trench to town and install a new cable myself in that time, I thought.

Reggie shrugged. "Exactly," said Mr Frost. "No use whatsoever. So drop into the new Reflection Room whenever you like and say what you really think. It's your secret, sacred space, no teachers allowed. Right then, Shiners, get back to your classes, and have fun!"

As we filed out I noticed a new sensor in the corner of the hall like the one we'd got at home. Mr Frost hadn't mentioned that.

Our class was near the old computer room so we were the first to get there at break. A new glossy black door barred the way with a hand sensor besides it like the bike racks. A metal plate had been installed above the door, engraved with words *Reflection Room*. Taped underneath was a scrawled sign: "Only one child at a time."

"I'm going in first," said Izzy, pushing the door.

I reached across her and put my hand on the sensor. "Welcome, Thora Batty," said an American voice.

"You lose, brain box."

With a *fssssh!* sound the door slid open, revealing... not much. In fact it was pitch black; it looked like you were stepping into space.

"Whoah," I said. This looked *very* dodgy.

"Go on then," said Izzy, smirking.

I looked around. I could see children pouring out of their classrooms now, all heading towards me, all wanting a look. I took a deep breath, and stepped forwards.

As soon as I was inside, the door behind me hissed closed. But just as I was about to panic, more doors slid open. The sight before me was so dizzying, so dazzling, I felt my knees go wobbly. A hundred children were staring at me from every angle: all around, all above. I held my hand to my eyes, and they did the same. I was surrounded by mirrors, as if I'd stepped inside a disco ball.

"Step forward, Thora." The voice was calm, but insistent.

After the doors had closed behind me the floor started to rotate. I no longer had any idea which way I was facing or where I'd come in. A school-full of Thoras frowned back at me.

I tried a smile and that made me feel better. I grinned, properly this time, and the world grinned with me. I pulled a face and stuck my tongue out, and was rewarded with a sight that would get an instant detention from Mrs Scott.

"What are you thinking today, Thora?"

I didn't know what to say to that. It also felt very weird,

speaking to myself.

"Umm. I dunno. That this is a bit strange?"

"Your thoughts are being heard," replied the voice.

"And I'm thinking that Charlie's brain will probably explode when he sees this," I added.

"Your thoughts are being heard," she said again.

I kept silent.

"If you need a thought starter, stamp your foot. To exit, jump," said the voice after a delay.

I stamped my right foot.

"What makes you happy?" asked the voice.

What an odd question. "Well... baked beans? And Flash Fried Fishy Feet. And The Chart Show. Also Izzy's new skipping rope."

I stamped again.

"What are you worried about?"

"Umm... how I'm going to get out of here?" I thought for a moment. "Also, I'm worried about Sheila, in hospital. And... when the telly channels are coming back on."

Stamp.

"What's the most fun you can have?"

That was just plain odd. "Well... when you get a bonus life on *Ogre Smackdown* for squishing the one in the bushes? [Silence.] When you're on multiplayer mode in *Race Max 2*? [More silence.] So what about when you're all on your bikes and the sun's shining and you've done all your homework? Am I right?"

"Your thoughts are being heard."

OK, enough already. I jumped. The floor stopped turning, and behind me a mirror slid sideways. I stepped through, and the mirrored room slid closed.

"Two house points awarded. Thank you Thora, have fun today."

Blinking in surprise, I was back out into the corridor.

"Well? What was it like?" asked Izzy excitedly. She was surrounded by children, all trying to be the next to get their hand onto the sensor.

"I'm not too sure. But I'm fairly sure my thoughts were heard."

When Reggie and I got home we went straight to the food cupboards: no biscuits, no sweets, no sugar of any kind. It had all been removed. Reggie found half an old choc ice in the freezer that had fallen out of the packet and tasted of pizza. We ate it anyway. It was so sweet, so delicious.

"What's going on, Reggie?" I asked, using a wet finger to extract the last cold shards of chocolate from the wrapper. "Why is school changing so much?"

"Maybe they're due for an inspection," said Reggie. He was pulling stuff out of the cupboards, looking for more sweet treats. "They always do extra stuff then, to make it look like they're really trying."

"Maybe. But not like this. Not getting Dad to chuck out all the custard creams. That's not just school, that's my *life*." The more I thought about it, the more I was beginning to feel quite indignant. Who asked me what I wanted – or any of us, for that matter? And what was in it for us?

"What are we going do now then, if we can't eat?"

"Cycle ride?"

'S'pose so."

We picked up bikes from the Play Park and looped around the roads of the village. We ended up on streets we didn't even know existed: that's the thing about cycling. Down one cul-de-sac, an old lady called out.

"Hello dearies!"

She was gardening, but leaning heavily on her walking frame.

"Hope you've had a lovely day at school," she said with a smile.

"Hi!" I said. "But I thought you..." But I trailed off. I didn't know how to ask politely. Because the gardening woman – who certainly wasn't in hospital having an operation and definitely wasn't about do cartwheels – was Sheila.

Chapter 16
LISTENING

FRIDAY, THE END of the first week back. And although it was only April, it was *roasting*. During the day we'd flapped our hands in class and fought over the water fountain in the playground. Even now, nearly seven o'clock, it was still warm enough to be out in our t-shirts. A warm breeze was blowing off the surrounding fells, earthy gusts of bracken and farm animals.

"Have you seen that?" Izzy hopped up next to me on the parked bikes, sitting backwards on the saddle and resting her feet on the knobbly tyres. She pointed over at the climbing equipment. "Boys really are disgusting."

Reggie was leaning down from the Witch's Hat and dribbling onto Charlie, who was trying to roll out of the way before the spit hit him.

"My mum says it's in their genes," she continued. "They're born to be revolting, they can't help it. It's like when a dog rolls in fox poo."

A glistening globule fell down, but Charlie didn't move fast enough. He wiped Reggie's saliva off his face with his t-shirt before lying down for another go.

"Gross," I said. "What took you so long, anyway?"

"Mum had to do tea on the cooker, so it took longer,"

said Izzy. "She said the microwave broke, but we won't bother getting another one."

"We haven't got a microwave," I said. "Dad won't have one in the house."

"Why not?"

"Well it used to be because of all the free food he could get from work, 'coz that goes straight in the oven. But Melissa has stopped him bringing that home now. She says it's packed with hidden sugar and we'll make our own."

Izzy shook her head. "That's bad news. Mum only used the microwave for vegetables anyway," said Izzy. "And she says we should eat more raw food."

I made a mental note not to go round to Izzy's for tea any time soon.

There was no point going home until Shannon or Melissa came to get us, because there was nothing on telly. Dad had put the games console away because he said it needed a software update, and without the internet he couldn't download it. We'd tried going to Enid's house after school. We hadn't been there for a while, and it ponged even worse than usual: a musty, almost fruity smell hung heavy in the dusty air. The heat was tremendous, and trapped flies buzzed and tapped at the windows.

We didn't have anything to do when we got there, either. Charlie and Reggie had fought over a sherbet double dipper that Charlie had saved up from before the sweet ban and sprayed it over Enid's lounge carpet. And Izzy said she was fed up of clearing up other people's mess, and stormed out.

So we'd ended up back at the play park, and half the village had clearly had the same idea.

"Where's Shannon?" asked Izzy, who had joined us

after she'd had her tea and calmed down.

"She's at home. It's her birthday tomorrow, so she's calling everyone to organise stuff."

It turned out that Shannon's birthday needed a *lot* of organising, even though she was only catching the bus into town with her friends.

Earlier that week Melissa, Dad, Reggie and I had been watching a documentary about chameleons on telly. Shannon put her head round the door.

"Dad? Can I have my phone back please?"

"We've discussed this already, Shannon," said Dad, not looking up. "Maybe 182 times. It's not happening."

"But I need to call people," she pleaded. "Nobody knows what's happening on Saturday. It's going to be a disaster."

"I think that's a bit melodramatic," said Melissa. "This might sound like a crazy plan, but you could always speak to them tomorrow, at school."

Shannon ignored her. "Dad, come on! Alice needs to sort her lift out, Tara needs to borrow my top, and Zoe isn't even sure she can make it."

Dad looked at Melissa.

"This is ridiculous," said Shannon. "I'm going to be eighteen, for God's sake. I could get a tattoo, or drive a lorry, or be an MP and stuff. But you won't even let me phone my friends?"

"I suppose we could set up the landline again," said Dad. "It's still connected. It's allowed, I checked."

"John, we've spoken about this..." protested Melissa. Dad waved her down.

"What's a landline?" asked Reggie.

"What's a landline," repeated Dad, shaking his head and levering himself off the sofa. "You kids don't know you're born."

"He means that rubbish old phone that used to be in the hall," I said. Dad had unplugged the house phone after Mum died, when people kept calling to say they didn't know what to say.

So that's how Shannon ended up at the bottom of the stairs every night that week, her hand cupped over her mouth as she spoke to her friends. The same friends she spent all day with at school.

The phone itself was red plastic, with buttons that used to be white but were now yellow. Dad plugged it in next to the front door. It wasn't even cordless; the handset was joined to the base by a curly wurly flex. Shannon twirled her fingers in it as she spoke, like she usually did with her hair. Every time we passed she scowled and stopped talking until we'd gone.

Back in the play park I was surprised to see Dad strolling towards us. "I got away early," he said, giving me a hug.

Izzy took that as her cue to head for home, but Reggie and Charlie weren't so keen.

"I got until half past," said Charlie. "Mum says so."

"We're playing Top Thumps," said Reggie, giving Charlie a dead leg.

"We'll hang here then, 'til you're all thumped out," said Dad, and we sat on one of the benches next to the fort, under the new lights. They flickered on as we sat down.

Dad asked me how I was doing. So I told him all about our first week back: how Film Club had been cancelled, about the new school dinner menu that meant it was now impossible to avoid fresh vegetables, about how I was thinking of joining the new Gymnastics Society, and about the Reflection Room. Everyone had stopped using it by day three, so they had to start promising an extra ten minutes of play if you went in.

"Lots going on then," said Dad. We sat in silence.

"You're happy, aren't you Thora?" asked Dad, out of the blue.

"I guess so," I said. "It's hard to say, sometimes."

"How do you mean?"

"Well... " I twisted so that I wasn't looking at Dad. Sometimes it's easier to talk that way. "I like Melissa and everything, but I still wish she was Mum. I think about her a lot, Dad. Do you?"

"I do, love. Every day. I expect I always will." We said nothing, just sat. "She'd have loved all this, though," he said, waving his hand.

"What, the play park?"

"Not just that. You lot, playing out here, riding bikes around the village, disappearing into... secret places. That's got to be fun, right?"

I decided to ignore the bit about secret places. "It would be more fun if we could play *Race Max 2* again," I said.

Dad chuckled.

"Dad?" I said. "What does FF really mean?"

"What?" he said. "FF? What's that? Why do you ask?"

"Come on, it's everywhere, I said. "It was on that poster at the school meeting, it was on our Play Packs, it's even on the bike racks."

"You've always been the inquisitive one," said Dad. He ran his hands through his hair, or what was left of it, and scratched his chin. I could hear the bristles rasping, like a sheep ripping up grass. "You're like your mother. She'd have been so proud of you."

"But you know, don't you, Dad?"

"I guess I do," he said. "But before I tell you – "

Dad was interrupted by an electrical whine. A white golf buggy was zipping towards us across the park, cutting straight across the grass and the paths until it came to a stop on the other side of the fort. At the wheel was the unmistakable figure of Mr Wharton. He unfolded himself and strode towards us with Kristi trotting along in his wake. With legs half as long as Mr Wharton she was struggling to keep up, and that was making it hard for her to keep that toothy grin going, too.

"Mr Batty!" hollered Mr Wharton. "Good evening!" He wasn't even close yet, but his old-fashioned newsreader voice could be heard across the park. "And what a *splendid* evening it is!" He reached the bench and shook Dad's hand. Dad nodded, and muttered hello. "And *here's* Thora, our little ambassador!" he boomed, turning to me. "Quite the bright young thing."

"Hi Flora!" said Kristi, who was hopping from one foot to another. "So good to meet your dad, too." She flashed a proper, all-the-lights-on smile at Dad.

"It's Thora," I mumbled.

Mr Wharton breathed in theatrically. "What a beautiful night to be out," he said. "Great to spend a bit of 'quality time' with the youngsters, as they say." A bead of sweat was running down his cheek.

"We're just having a Friday chat," said Dad. "Catching up."

"Yes, I could *see* that very well," said Mr Wharton. "Couldn't we, Kristi?"

"Oh yes," she said. "We spotted it straight away."

"Well I'm so sorry for interrupting you," said Mr Wharton. It's a bit late for that, I thought. "You've probably forgotten what you were talking about! Silly old me!" He threw back his head and laughed so hard I wondered if I'd misheard. Perhaps I'd missed a great joke, although Dad wasn't laughing. Kristi tittered away besides him, but I wasn't sure she knew what she was laughing at, either.

"Yes, we're probably done here," said Dad, taking my hand and getting up. "Time for us to get home."

"That's the spirit," said Mr Wharton, clapping Dad hard on the back. Dad's hand tensed, his fingers squeezing mine hard.

"Do stay on the right path, won't you Mr Batty?" said Mr Wharton, looking directly at Dad. "We can't have people heading off in any direction, oh deary me, no. That would *never* do." He held his arms out, as if to usher us home. "Lovely to see you both, do have fun this evening, won't you?"

"Night night, Dora!" twittered Kristi.

"Good night, Kirsty," I said, as we walked away.

"Oh, no!" she protested. "It's not Kirsty, it's – "

But by that point I couldn't hear her. Dad gave me

another squeeze and I could see he was smiling. We waved at Reggie who gave Charlie one last thump and then ran across to join us.

"What was that all about?" I asked. I looked back: the buggy was whizzing off to the exit, cutting across the grass again. "And why is he so bothered about *us* staying on the right path?"

"He's a buffoon," said Dad. "He thinks he's important, but he's not."

"Hey, there's Melissa!" said Reggie.

And sure enough, there she was, standing at the railings, watching us approach. Except that it took her a second to realise that we were looking in her direction. And in that moment, before she turned on a smile, I saw a hard-lined expression I hadn't seen before. Business-like, the face of a woman who doesn't like what she sees.

Chapter 17
SHADOWS

AS FAST AS it had begun, the hot spell ended. Barely a day old. As old people never tire of saying in our part of the world, *if you don't like the weather now, wait a few minutes.* A rumble of thunder out of a blue sky was the first omen; we're so low in the valley that we don't see the weather until it's right on top of us.

The first fat splashes on the pavements almost fizzed, vapour rising from the hot road. Children ran for cover but the rain petered out. "This weather is all mouth and no trousers," said Dad, looking up as we arrived back at the house. "Maybe it'll bucket down later on."

And it did. I woke up with a jerk, heart pounding. There was an unusual smell; a damp, after-the-rain, something-happened-when-you-were-asleep kind of whiff.

Across the room I could hear Reggie shuffling in his sleep, his breath whirring gently, a comforting noise like the flutter of pigeons' wings in a town square after someone claps their hands. He changed position again and high up in the corner a red light blinked.

My heartbeat slowed to a steady thump-thud, a water wheel set to idle, my nightie soaked with sweat.

But then, out there in the darkness, I heard something.

It was a fleeting wisp of noise, so delicate that every time I tried to bring it into focus it seemed to melt away. But in the gaps between Reggie's sighs and murmurs, when I pretended not to listen, it was there: the unmistakable sound of people laughing.

I swung my legs out of bed and padded around the room, trying to work out where it was coming from.

When I was small, not long after my Mum died, Dad once became convinced that someone had left a radio on. He beckoned Reggie and me into rooms to listen, and sure enough we could hear tinny laughter. It seemed to get louder when we crouched down. "I think it's the pipes," said Dad. "They must be picking up a signal."

Even then, Shannon was sharp in every way.

"Radio? In the pipes?" She stood next to Dad, listening. And then she slapped him on the leg. "It's your phone. You've left your podcast on."

Dad had pulled out his talking phone, and smiled. "Ah, my charming daughter has solved another mystery. I don't know what I'd do without you all." And he held us tightly for a long, long time.

But it wasn't a phone this time. Or a TV. Not in this valley, not since The Changes.

The sound seemed loudest by my bed, near the wall. But Enid's house hadn't heard any laughter apart from our own for many years, not since Enid was there. And even then she wasn't exactly the laughing type.

I sat on the edge of my bed. What woke me? It was a mystery. I'll ask Izzy about it in the morning, I thought, or Dad when he gets home at lunchtime.

Getting cold, I slid my feet back into the warmth under

114

the covers. But a sharp scrunch stopped me dead: the sound of shoe on gravel. Back on my feet, I ran across to the window in three huge leaps, slamming my hands against the window frame. It was nearly pitch black outside: the moon had retreated behind a cloud. I peered through the glass and was just about to give up when a silhouette on the path beneath me caught me eye.

For a second the figure paused and bounced on its toes, as if judging the distance. Then it took a handful of easy strides and vaulted the gate, swinging a laptop case high into the air. There was only one grown-up in this house who carries a laptop case, and it wasn't Dad.

Only then did I notice the void beyond the gate. It is so hard to describe – like a missing jigsaw piece, as if someone had cut out a black hole in the landscape. But on this dark night you could see it because it was actually *too* black; the pavement, trees and road beyond were grey by comparison.

Then, to my utter astonishment, Melissa climbed straight into the hole. She was completely swallowed up by the darkness. And with the *shlick* of tyres on wet tarmac, the inky cut-out slid out of view.

Chapter 18
BORED

THE NEXT MORNING was Shannon's 18th birthday and it started with eggy bread. While Melissa cooked, Dad bopped balloons around the kitchen and Reggie kept asking when Shannon could open her presents.

The first was a bulky, lumpy thing propped up against the wall.

"Cost me a tenner in wrapping paper, that did," said Dad as Shannon ripped into it, revealing a rucksack big enough for a small child. Or indeed a medium-sized child, as Reggie proved by climbing in.

"Erm, yeah, thanks Dad," said Shannon.

"Ahem!" said Dad, nodding at Melissa.

"Oh, yeah, you too Melissa, thanks."

"Try the envelope."

We all watched as she tore into it, pulling out a card with a picture of a beach on the front. "Whoah," she said, reading it. "Is this...? No, it can't be serious. Dad!"

"What is it, Shannon?" I asked.

"Seriously! Dad! No way!"

Dad smiled, and put his arm round Melissa.

"Shannon, what is it?"

"That is *amazing!* Oh-my-God Oh-my-God Oh-my-

God Oh-my-God!"

"Shannon! TELL ME!" I couldn't wait, and grabbed the voucher.

Flight Time Ltd
Round The World Ticket: 1 passenger
The "Triple A" Experience
Africa, Asia and the Americas

"Seriously, I have to tell Alice," said Shannon, grabbing it back, and rushing to the phone in the hall. It didn't take long before we heard screaming and she came rushing back.

"Dad! Alice has got one too!"

Dad sliced another banana onto his eggy bread. "Well, what are the chances, eh?"

"You knew, didn't you! And you never told me!"

"I *might* have had a word with Alice's dad," he said.

"So awesome," said Shannon, disappearing back into the hall to shriek down the phone at someone else.

How quickly a day can turn sour, though. Heavy, stop-start rain had arrived in earnest. Wet play. Reggie and I sat on our bedroom floor playing with dominos that Melissa had bought, raising our voices to be heard above the rain on the window and occasional rumbles of thunder.

"What are you doing?" I heard Shannon say, somewhere outside on the landing.

"I was just – " That was Melissa's voice, muffled

through the wall.

"You shouldn't be in there. Nobody goes in there."

"I was uncovering it. It shouldn't be covered, the system doesn't work properly." Melissa's voice was louder now as she came out of Shannon's bedroom.

I knew exactly what she was talking about, because I'd noticed it too: Shannon had wrapped a t-shirt over the alarm sensor in her room.

"It can't detect movement with that on, that's all," said Melissa.

Reggie's hand froze in mid-air with a double four domino, and I realised I was holding my breath.

"That's all? You must really think I'm stupid," said Shannon.

"Oh come on, Shannon, don't be such a drama queen."

"I know what's going on," said Shannon. "And *that's* an invasion of my privacy."

Reggie frowned at me. I shrugged.

"You might not like it, but it's all approved and above board," said Melissa, as if that was the final word.

"Aren't you forgetting something? I don't know if you've noticed, but I'm an adult now. I could sue you."

"Oh, come on – " Melissa stopped, mid sentence.

"I'm right, aren't I? I can tell by your face."

There was a moment's silence. You could almost *hear* Shannon's hands on her hips. "You don't think I know what you're up to, but I do. And I'm going to make sure everyone else knows too, starting now."

"Wait! It's... well it's complicated," said Melissa said. Her voice was softer now, less bossy.

"Well come on then, I'm all ears," said Shannon.

"Not here. It's not the place. Let's go for a walk."

"What, out there? It's lashing down! Where would we go?"

"Come on, I'll take the big umbrella. We won't go far. There's some people you should meet."

"This had better be good," said Shannon. I heard her clomping down the stairs – she was wearing her big boots in the house again. Melissa's lighter footsteps followed.

There was a moment's silence.

"Double four," said Reggie, "beat that. Come on, can you go or can't you? What are you waiting for?"

I let Reggie beat me at dominos; I was too busy thinking about what I'd heard. We tried and failed to work out how to play Chinese Checkers (another Melissa present). We did play-fighting, until Reggie hit me too hard and it turned into a real fight, and he started crying. Reggie went to watch TV but came back said it was just "dumb programmes for old people." He started to build domino towers; I wasn't interested. I squeaked my fingertip down the window instead, tracing the path of the raindrops. I thought about doing my homework, but not for very long. I got an itch on my back, so I tried to scratch it with a ruler. I was utterly, beyond-a-joke bored.

The doorbell rang – rescue at last. But it was only Charlie.

"Is Reggie there?"

"Yeah, I'm here," called Reggie.

"Wanna come to the park? They've set up a play tent."

Dad came downstairs. "Hey Charlie, how're you? How's your Mum and Dad?"

"Good thanks, Mr Batty," said Charlie. "I've done my homework so Mum says I can play."

"Good for you," said Dad, lacing up his trainers. We didn't even know he had any trainers until he started cycling, and now he was running, too. No prizes for guessing who gave him that idea.

"Where's Shannon?" I asked.

"She's gone out with Melissa," said Dad, leaning with both hands against the wall to stretch his legs.

"I know that, but where's she gone?"

"Haven't got a clue," said Dad, his voice straining. "Can't imagine they'll be long, though, Shannon's going into town soon for her birthday shindig."

He jogged up and down a couple of times. "Right, I'm ready. Don't do anything daft, and see you later."

With nothing better to do, I followed the boys along to the play park. The rain had spluttered to a halt, but menacing clouds rolled overhead and the park was nearly empty.

Two women were sitting on deckchairs under a white gazebo. Boxes of chalks were scattered around; Reggie and Charlie ran off with one, laughing. Kristi was there too, showing Year 1 children how to play hopscotch. A bunch of Year 5 girls stood in a circle with a loop of elastic around their knees, chanting while another girl skipped.

Charlie Chaplin sat on a pin
How many inches did it go in?
One, two, three, four.

A woman in a red t-shirt who seemed to be helping them beckoned me over but I shook my head because I recognised one of the women at the table: it was Sheila, the lollipop lady.

"Hey Thora!" she said, patting a chair for me to sit down. "Come and join us! Me and Margaret here could do with some company." I didn't have a clue who Margaret was but she smiled, and returned to her knitting.

"Hi Sheila. What are you doing here?"

"Well, Margaret is here to teach the youngsters street dancing, and I'm in charge of skydiving. Isn't that right, Marge?"

"That's the plan, Sheila," Margaret replied, without looking up. "Not many customers, though."

"No, but seriously?"

"Well, they thought it would be a good idea for us oldies to show you how to have fun, some games you might not know. And since I've got a bit of time on my hands... " Sheila smiled.

"*Who* thought it would be a good idea?"

Margaret looked up at her from her knitting with a frown.

"Oh don't look at me like that, you silly old stick. It can't do any harm to tell them. It's your headmaster, Mr Frost." Sheila paused. "And that government fellow, Mr Horton, Gorton, or whatever his name is."

"Wharton," I said. "The one with all the arms and legs."

"That's the chappie!" said Sheila. Margaret tutted.

"What kind of games, anyway?" I asked.

"Take a look," she said, pointing at the table in front of her. An array of labelled plastic pots and containers filled the table. I could see marbles, skipping ropes, tiddlywinks, dice, metal jacks and more.

"Can you show me games with these?" I said, holding up some coloured rubber quoits.

"Maybe not today," said Sheila, "my hip isn't enjoying this damp weather."

"I though you were having it fixed? Mr Wharton said you were. That's why we've got the new woman," I said, pointing to Kristi.

"And she's rubbish," added Reggie, back for more chalk. "She won't let us cross unless we walk next to her and talk really loudly. One day she said she got something wrong, and she made us cross the road and say the same things all over again. Why can't we have you back?"

Shelia looked at Margaret, who pursed her lips and shook her head slightly. Sheila sighed.

"They've... they've given me a new date for the operation. I'm having a bit of time off."

"What about you, Margaret?" I asked. "Will you play quoits with me?"

Sheila laughed. "Margaret? I haven't seen her run since 1952." Margaret ignored her, and me. "Why don't you ask Kristi?"

"Nah," I said. "I'll stay here with you."

"In that case, let's play Cat's Cradle."

Sheila fished some string from one of the tubs. I stuck out my fingers and Sheila patiently taught me how to make Cat's Eye, Fish in a Dish, Soldier's Bed and Manger.

After an hour or so Sheila bundled up the string and passed it over. Drops of rain were pattering onto the gazebo. "You keep it, dear, I need to head for home. I'm seizing up, and I think it's coming on for another downpour."

Sheila pushed down on the chair and slowly got to her feet.

"When will you be our lollipop lady again?" I asked. I looked over at Kristi, who was now playing tag with some children I didn't recognise.

Sheila smiled. "It's harder than it seems, that job," she said. "Though maybe not as hard as she makes it look. And I'll be back, as soon as this is all over."

Margaret coughed. "When your hip operation is finished, you mean, Sheila."

"Yes, of course," said Sheila, sounding flustered. "When my op is over. That's right." She raised a walking stick and pointed at the dark clouds. "Don't you children catch a cold, now. Or you too, Margaret; you know what a grump you are when you're poorly."

Margaret raised her hand in farewell as Sheila shuffled off towards the gate.

Izzy was crouched down with Reggie and Charlie, playing noughts and crosses. I said goodbye and ran across to join them.

"We need to go," I told them, "or we'll get soaked."

"No point coming back to mine," said Izzy. "Our telly is on the blink, it's gone black and white."

"So has ours," said Reggie.

"What are you talking about?" I said.

"It's true, I told you," he said, pulling his jumper over his head to keep the rain off. "All the programmes are for old people."

"No, stupid, it's the same programmes, there's just no colour," said Izzy, but she should have saved her breath because the boys had already run ahead.

"Izzy, I don't like it," I said as we trotted along.

"Me neither. I watched Dragon Boat Races, and I couldn't even tell which team was blue and which team was red."

"No, not that," I replied. "Everything. It's all changing and going wrong. The internet. Phones. Games. The TV. Your microwave. Everything has stopped working."

"I just play more chess," said Izzy.

"Something's definitely not right." I stopped. "And do you know the strangest thing?"

"Ah yes, I know this one," said Izzy. "I found out last night. Pizza Presto won't deliver any more. Yesterday was the first Friday of the month and we always have pizza on the first Friday, so my dad called them, but they said they won't drive up the valley. They said they've been told by their boss they can't deliver to our village."

I scratched my head. I certainly wasn't thinking of pizza. Although Izzy comes top of every test we have, I sometimes wonder if she's on the same planet as the rest of us.

"No, not that," I said, "though that's a bit weird, too. But haven't you noticed?" Our trot was now a full-on sprint, and we squinted to keep the rain out of our eyes. I shouted across to make myself heard. "Izzy! It's all going massively wrong, so why does nobody seem to mind?"

Chapter 19
BACK TO ENID'S HOUSE

THE RAIN WAS pelting down by the time we got back to my house. The boys were huddled on the doorstep when we panted up to join them. But we could barely all fit on the step, and the small overhang above the door wasn't keeping the rain off.

"It's locked!" said Reggie, stating the obvious as always, and ringing on the doorbell like crazy. "And so's the back door!"

This wasn't the first time this had happened since Melissa arrived. If there was a lock, you could be sure she used it: on her briefcase, her laptop, her phone (when she still had it – she'd given it up like everyone else), and our front door, too. "I'm sorry," she had said, "force of habit. In London, you need to lock everything."

We weren't in London now, but we were still locked out.

"Quick, next door!" I shouted, and we made a run for it. We ducked under the low branches of the cherry tree by the gate and up the path, long sodden grass whipping at our legs. Izzy was first to burst through Enid's back door, with the rest of us tumbling after. I slammed it shut behind us and we flopped down onto the living room sofas.

"I'm soaked," said Reggie, running his hands through his hair and throwing his wet jumper down.

"Me too," Charlie added, tugging at his shorts. "Right down to my pants. It feels like I've wet myself."

Izzy wrinkled her nose in disgust and plucked at her t-shirt. "It stinks in here. When will someone get back to let us in?"

"Dunno," I said. "Dad might be ages, it depends how long his run is. Shannon will have gone into town by now, and Melissa, well..."

"She's probably out on one of her secret missions," said Reggie, leaning across to give Charlie another whack. Their game of Top Thumps clearly wasn't over.

"What secret missions?" asked Izzy. I was glad she asked, because it meant I didn't have to.

"The ones she does at night. When she's out doing her spying. Ow!" Reggie rubbed his arm, and Charlie leapt away before he could get revenge.

"Is Melissa really a spy?" Izzy asked me.

I opened my mouth to speak, but you can only speak when you have something to say. I didn't. Imagine tackling a tricky maths problem, and then someone walks past and slips an answer onto your desk. But is it the answer to *your* problem? Was that the reason for all these changes? Could it be that easy? Because life's not normally like that.

And if it *was* Melissa, what on earth did that mean? That would make my first problem look like a lift-the-flap picture book.

"Well, I guess..."

"Of course she is," interrupted Reggie, who was looking up at the windows. "She goes out after we're in bed, trying not to make any noise. Nobody knows what she does, not even Dad. And she works for that red dot spying company too," he said with a grunt as he climbed onto the back of the sofa.

My head was spinning. I felt completely out of control, like someone else was making up the rules. Reggie wasn't supposed to know more than me! And here he was, standing on the windowsill staring up at the windows, spouting all this spying stuff about Melissa. I needed to show them that I knew stuff, too.

"The red spots are everywhere," I said. "They were on the van that fitted our burglar alarm, and the truck with the Village Bikes, and that piece of paper I found in the park."

"And the golf buggies," added Izzy.

"And Melissa's laptop," added Reggie, reaching up on tiptoes while Charlie thumped his legs, trying to make him fall over.

"What?" I couldn't help myself.

"There's a sticker, on the bottom," he said. He looked at me. "How else would we know she's the spy?"

"Oh yes," I said, "I forgot." I needed a moment to think about this. "What are you doing, Reggie?"

"I'm trying to reach that window," he said. "The rain's coming in. Look, the carpet's getting wet."

He was right. One of the small top windows was ajar; water was dribbling onto the windowsill and dripping onto the carpet, turning one of the big swirly orange flowers a dark brown colour. I climbed up besides Reggie. Elbowing him out of the way, I yanked the small window shut.

That would explain how the swarms of flies from yesterday had escaped, but that wasn't what I was thinking about. None of us had opened that window – not today, not yesterday, never. Children don't open windows "for a bit of fresh air", it's not something we think about.

Could windows fall open? I guess in an old house, anything can happen. But for now, I didn't say anything. This was secret knowledge, and I had a lot of catching up to do.

Reggie jumped from the window sill onto the sofa with a shout, catching Charlie by surprise. They rolled off onto the floor.

"So what's she spying on then?" asked Izzy, sounding one-out-of-ten interested. If I had to guess, I reckon she thought that this was a definitely a 'boy' problem.

Reggie stopped rolling on the floor for a moment. "What? Or who? No idea. Dad? Shannon? Thora? Who cares?" And that was it: he was lost in the game again.

"She's not actually a spy, is she Thora?" asked Izzy. "My Dad reads spy books and there's always blood on the cover, or a knife or something."

"It's hard to say," I said, thinking quickly. "Maybe she's trying to work out who's turning everything off and making everything go wrong. She's trying to catch a baddie." This was starting to make sense (maybe).

"What, like James Bond?"

"Yeah, except she's Jane Bond." I was pretty pleased with that.

Izzy paused, thinking. "Why would anyone want to turn our telly black and white?"

"Baddies aren't stupid. It could be part of their evil plan," I announced, though even I would admit it seemed like a very strange plan.

We sat in silence for a moment, watching the boys fight. "What are we going to do?" she asked.

"We should watch her, in case she needs any help," I said. I was starting to feel much more in control now.

"What, like spy on the spy?"

"Exactly. Keep her under surveillance."

"That word again," said Izzy.

"Like a police stake-out," said Reggie's muffled voice from under Charlie's bottom.

"Uh-huh," I said, not wanting to encourage Reggie to share any more of his espionage tidbits.

"Keep going boys, you're cleaning up all the sherbet," said Izzy. She was right: as they rolled around on the floor, all the sherbet that Charlie had spilled the day before was sticking to their damp clothes.

"Let's help them," I said, and we jumped down and rolled the giggling bundle of Charlie and Reggie across the white powder.

"Just a bit more to get in the corner," said Izzy, trying to turn them around the sofa by the bottom of the staircase. "Left a bit, right a bit... "

"Wait!" I shouted.

"What?" replied half of our human sticky roller.

"Look! There!" I pointed at the bottom step, the one before the locked door. "Do you see?"

The others looked. "Sherbet," said Charlie, preparing to sit down and finish his cleaning job with his bottom.

Izzy held him back. "No, I see it," she said. "That's... "

"That's a clue," I said. In fact it was two clues, because outlined perfectly in sherbet were two footprints: the treads of a big heavy footstep, and a smaller, narrower one alongside.

Footprints? Spies? Red spots? What was going on? Whatever it was, it seemed to be happening right under my nose. And the worst thing was that without the internet, I couldn't even Google it.

At that moment I caught sight of Melissa through the window, walking up our garden path. Izzy rushed off home for tea. I gave Charlie a gentle push after her, towards the door. "You too, Charlie," I said. Charlie 'needs instructions', as teachers say. One more thump from Reggie and Charlie was gone.

As I was pulling the door closed behind us, I paused.

"Reggie, does all this sound normal to you? Do you think anything bad is going to happen?"

"It already has," Reggie said. "I haven't been able to play *Race Max 2* for weeks."

"No, worse than that," I said, though I could see by his face he couldn't imagine anything much worse.

Reggie shrugged.

"You know, with Melissa," I prompted. "With her being a spy and everything."

"I dunno," said Reggie. "It's a mystery. It's supposed to be a mystery, all spy stories are."

If I wanted reassurance, I wasn't going to get it from Reggie. This was like getting blood out of a stone. "Anyway, why all the questions?" he continued. "You sound like Melissa, or that woman in the Reflection Room," he said. He was right, I did. "Anyway, I'm not worried. I bet lots of people live with spies, they just don't know it. As long as we're OK, and Dad's OK, then there's nothing to worry about. And the new bikes are pretty cool."

My stomach lurched. I hadn't given Dad a second thought. Did he even know about Melissa? Surely he wasn't a spy, too?

"Is that what you told the Reflection Room?"

Reggie laughed. "Are you joking? You know that Frosty is listening to every word you say, don't you? They've probably got a TV in the staff room and everything." Reggie broke free and ran off, still smiling.

I paused, lost in thought. Was Mr Frost running a spy ring? It was possible, though I'd never seen him show much interest in anything except the colour of his jackets and his terrible jokes. And even if he was, who was he spying on, and why? It was all so confusing.

What's more, I seemed to be the only one who felt it was a problem worth solving.

Chapter 20
WHO SPIES ON THE SPIES?

I CAUGHT UP with Reggie at the front door. "Hello!" we both shouted as we elbowed our way into the hall. Melissa was in the kitchen, working on her laptop. (She was allowed because 'work screens' didn't count in the ban, apparently.) In one smooth movement she closed the lid and got up to greet us, but I was ready for this and managed to catch sight of her screen first. Unfortunately it had a big graph on it with loads of numbers and not, as I hoped, spy shots of the enemy.

"Hi guys, did you have fun at the park?"

"We were locked out!" said Reggie, rummaging in the cupboard for something to eat.

"Oops," she said. "Sorry about that. I can't stop myself."

"Where did you go?" I asked. "Dad's gone out for a run."

"I was dropping Shannon off at the bus stop. She was worried about the rain spoiling her birthday hair," Melissa said, a little unkindly. "Anyway, tea will be about an hour, so don't you go filling yourselves up. I've done a nice moussaka. You know, baked aubergines."

Reggie's face said it all.

"Reggie... "

"Why can't we have something out of the freezer?"

"Because we shouldn't be eating all that processed food," said Melissa. "It's like they told you in assembly. It's not... well it's not natural."

"Aubergines aren't natural," said Reggie. "Anything that turns to mush when you cook it isn't natural."

"You'll love it," said Melissa. "And anyway, what's all that white stuff on your clothes?"

"Oh yeah, it's... "

"It's chalk," I interrupted. "From the games in the park."

"And it's all over your back because... ? No, don't answer that, I don't want to know. Now get out of this kitchen while I make us a nice salad to go with it."

Reggie made another face and we headed for the lounge. We were about to plonk ourselves down when Melissa shouted through from the kitchen. "And no sitting on the sofa until you've both got changed!"

You had to admit, she was sharp. But then I guess only the brightest people go to spy academy.

"Check it out," said Reggie as we left the room. "Almost done."

He was pointing at HOUSE 2.0, and he was right: Dad had been busy with his magic markers. All the windows were now solid ink. A carefully shaded soil pipe had been fitted under the toilet outlet. The upstairs windows had curtains (tied back); downstairs there were blinds (fastened up). A bed was visible in one of the rooms, complete with a United duvet cover (that must be Reggie's). It wasn't quite complete – the kitchen was still empty, for example – but suddenly this looked like a house you could live in, not a child's drawing before the colouring in begins.

"Wow," I said. "Where has he got all the money from?"

"Dunno," said Reggie. "Extra shifts?"

I hadn't noticed Dad being at work more than usual. In fact it seemed to me as if he was around more, not less. Maybe he'd got a promotion.

"I can't see a TV," said Reggie, peering at the lounge.

"Probably doesn't think it's worth bothering when there's nothing on," I said.

"I'm not fussed, anyway," said Reggie, heading for the door. "I'd rather go out on my bike."

And with a slam of the front door, he was gone.

Dad returned soon afterwards and an hour later we were all sitting down to dinner: all except Shannon, of course. I was surprisingly hungry and the moussaka was surprisingly nice. For a moment, there was quiet.

"Not bad," said Dad. "Not bad at all. Not as good as one of ours, of course, but... "

"Oi," said Melissa. "I bet your version is called something ridiculous, too."

"Not at all," said Dad, taking another forkful. "It's called Magic Mushy Mouthfuls. Not one of our biggest sellers, I'll admit."

"With a name like that, I'm not exactly surprised."

"I'll ignore that," said Dad. "Especially because I think I came up with it. Anyway, what've you all been up to while I was getting drenched?"

Reggie told Dad about the games in the park, but I gave him a kick under the table when he started to talk about what we did next, and interrupted.

"And then it was raining, so we came home, but we couldn't get in because Melissa had locked the door."

Melissa made an *oops* face, while Dad shook his head and tutted. "She'll learn. Her big city ways aren't needed around here. We must be the safest village in the country."

"Especially with all the new burglar alarms," added Reggie.

"And the surveillance," I added, testing the waters. I wanted to see what Melissa would do. Dad raised his eyebrows at me, but Melissa simply picked up the serving spoon.

"Now then, any more for any more?"

It was dark now, and my mind was whirring. We had gone to bed a bit later than usual because Dad and Melissa had been arguing, and neither of us wanted to go downstairs to say goodnight. It was angry whispers, mostly, interrupted by the sounds of washing up. Occasionally Dad's voice rose as he forgot to whisper. "You say *stand firm*, but it's gone beyond a joke," I heard him say at one point. "That's not the life I want, and it's not what the kids want, either."

But it was only occasional phrases, and it was hard to make sense of it all. When the last words seem to have been said, we crept downstairs. Dad was sat on the sofa, his arm outstretched, cycling between the three TV channels endlessly, as if one of them might burst into colour or even look slightly interesting.

Seeing us, he beckoned us over.

"It's all rubbish," said Reggie.

"Yeah," he said. "We'd do a better job ourselves, I reckon." He turned off the telly.

"Do you think we'll ever be back to normal?" asked Reggie.

Dad didn't say anything. "Is that what you want?" He pulled Reggie onto his lap.

I heard a sound and looked round. Melissa was standing quietly at the door. Dad spotted her, but looked quickly back at Reggie.

"Not sure," said Reggie. "Some of it's OK, I guess. The bikes. The new stuff at school."

"The play park," I added. Reggie nodded.

"But?" prompted Dad. Melissa made to move forward, but Dad gave her another look.

"But... we used to have loads of fun together," said Reggie. "Watching TV. Games. *Race Max 2*. All that stuff. And now you're at work, or we're in the park."

Dad gave Reggie a squeeze. "Yeah," he said. "I know what you mean. It'll all come right, I promise."

"Promise?" Reggie looked up at Dad, who reached out and pulled me into his bundle.

"Promise. Now get yourselves to bed. Go on, scram. We'll need all our energy for Shannon tomorrow, she'll be like a bear with a sore head."

As we passed Melissa in the doorway she gave us both a quick kiss on the head. "Your Dad's right," she said. "Everything happens for a reason. See you in the morning."

In bed, my mind was spinning, thinking about those footprints in the sherbet. Even if one of them *was* Melissa, who was the other?

In the darkness, I heard Reggie shuffle; I knew he was still awake.

"We should measure the footprints," I said softly. "So we can check out people's shoes."

"Too late, they've already gone," murmured Reggie.

I jolted awake. "What are you talking about?"

"The footprints, they've been cleared up. Right, night night."

"No! Wait!" I said, sitting up. "What do you mean they've been cleaned up? Who cleaned them up?"

"I don't know, but I saw it through the window. And all the furniture's been moved around. I forgot my jumper so I went back to get it, but the door was locked."

I lay back down with a *whump* and stared up at the ceiling. A red light flashed in the corner. The more I thought about it, the less it all made sense, and the more tired I became.

I was on the edge of sleep when Reggie spoke again. "There she goes again," he said quietly. "Listen. Front door open... " There was a moment of silence, followed by an unmistakable metallic click. "Front door closed."

And then that soft electrical sound again, fading back into the night.

I fell into a troubled sleep, dreaming that I had gone up for an award at assembly. But as Frosty handed it over he laughed, and as he laughed his face melted, like wax. Underneath was Melissa, who was laughing too, and that set off the rest of the school. They fell about, uncontrollable, and I ran from the hall with my hands over my ears, out of the village and onto the fells. But as far as I ran, all I could hear was the laughter.

Chapter 21
SHANNON REINVENTED

REGGIE WAS ALREADY up when I woke the next morning, the duvet abandoned on the floor and the curtain yanked half open. I lay on my back, listening to the sounds of Sunday.

The church bell chimed half past, but half past what? I had no idea. After the rain of the previous day, it sounded as if small boys had been sent out for their exercise; shouts and yelps drifted across from the play park.

Downstairs I could hear Reggie chattering away, the clatter of pots and pans and the slow crescendo of the kettle coming to the boil. That would be Dad, getting ready for our Big Sunday Breakfast. Once or twice a month – whenever he didn't have a Sunday shift – we'd eat our cereal to the sound of bacon sizzling and spitting in the frying pan. Dad would race through his cornflakes and jump to his feet, fetching the dented white metal jug from the fridge.

One of the few things that didn't come from a packet, Dad's pancake batter was his pride and joy. He made it to his gran's recipe, whisking it into silky bubbles and leaving it to rest in the fridge overnight. As we ate he'd wait patiently for his square, cast iron skillet to heat up, holding a steady hand over it to test the temperature.

"We're off!" he'd say when the time was right. He poured the smooth, pale batter into the pan from shoulder height, raising and lowering the jug like a cocktail waiter. Five perfect discs would appear, positioned like spots on dice.

He'd turn his back on the pancakes while they cooked and chat to anybody who was up, leaning across to thwack Reggie with the spatula if he was being cheeky. Perhaps it was the rising smell of toasting pancakes or a change in the sizzle but he always knew exactly when to turn and flip the discs over, like counters on a board game. A short time later he'd slide the nut brown circles into the warm oven, heat the pan back up and start again. Five times over, 25 pancakes in total, slumped higgledy-piggledy on the oval plate alongside unruly crumples of rusty bacon.

This particular morning, as I lay in bed thinking about pancakes, there was an unexpected voice in the chatter that rose from the kitchen: Shannon. She rarely made it for breakfast. Normally, she'd slope down late in the morning and hunch over her cereal bowl, her long hair screening the view of her grumpy face as she tapped out SOS instant messages to her friends.

I swung my legs out of bed and padded downstairs. My hand rested for a moment on one of Reggie's jumpers drying over the banisters – it was the blue one, still damp from yesterday's rain. That's odd, I thought; Reggie said it was locked inside Enid's front room.

"Good morning, sleepy bones!" said Shannon as I entered the kitchen, rubbing my eyes. Shannon's hair was wrapped in a towel, her face still pink from the shower.

"We've been up for ages, haven't we Reggie?"

No grumpy faces here; clearly Shannon's birthday had been a success. I took a seat and poured myself some muesli. Melissa had brought that home.

Melissa was there too, sipping her coffee and flicking through a magazine while Dad worked his pancake magic. "Nearly done," he said, sliding the last batch onto the hot plate and placing it on the table.

That's when I noticed what was missing. "Where's the bacon, Dad?"

"We haven't got any," said Melissa, not looking up.

"It's not good for you to eat too much meat," said Shannon, reaching for the low fat yoghurt.

I did the same, and we tucked in. We chatted about Shannon's night out ("epic", but that's about as much as she'd say), Melissa's plan to restart her long distance running, and Reggie's upcoming sports day.

"What're you guys up to today?" asked Shannon. She tucked a stray lock of hair back under her towel and looked at me, expectantly.

"I... well I don't know," I said. "I guess I'll head over to the play park, maybe meet up with Izzy." It sounds a simple question, but I really wasn't used to it. Now that I thought about it, I couldn't remember the last time Shannon had asked me a question.

"You should get out on the Village Bikes," said Shannon, reaching for another pancake. "Maybe explore a bit, get some exercise."

"Yeah, well thanks for the fitness advice," I said. "Shame it has to come from someone who watches eight hours of telly every day."

"In black and white," added Reggie.

"Calm down, you two," warned Melissa.

But Shannon didn't react in any case. "Not me. I'm meeting friends," she said, though nobody had asked. "Does anyone want any more kiwi?"

Dad shook his head, though it was hard to know if that was because he'd had enough kiwi, or because he couldn't understand this 'new improved Shannon' who was eating breakfast with us.

"Charlie and me are going to do planes," said Reggie.

Dad peered out of the window at the white clouds scudding across the blue sky. "It might work," he said.

Doing planes meant that Reggie and Charlie would be heading for the path behind the church, the one up the side of the fell. Dad discovered long ago that if you climbed to the first bend there was a flat rock that made the perfect spot to launch a paper aeroplane. When you could feel the warmth of the sun on your face, if the wind was wafting gently in the right direction, and if you gave your plane a big throw... your plane would soar above the church and out over the village, rising and banking on the currents.

The back door opened, and Charlie barrelled in. "Morning Mr Batty! Morning Mrs Batty!" he said cheerily to Melissa.

Shannon shrieked with laughter, and then started to cough on a piece of kiwi.

"No, I'm not Mrs... " began Melissa, but Charlie started poking at the pancakes and clearly wasn't listening.

"There, there," said Dad, red with embarrassment and slapping her on the back harder than necessary. "Now then Charlie, help yourself to... ah. You already have."

"Gnugh fnishurgle," said Charlie, his cheeks bulging and fingers reaching out for more.

"Such charming manners," said Melissa with a grimace.

"Come on Charlie, let's make our planes," said Reggie.

"Hey, I'll help you," said Shannon.

For a second I wondered if I was hearing things. Shannon? Helping? The others were as shocked as me, judging by their reaction.

"What?" said Shannon. "I'm great at making planes. We could colour them red or something, so they're easier to see."

Dad raised his eyebrows and smiled.

"Don't forget your plates!" he shouted as they tried to leave the room. Reggie shuffled back to collect his bowl and cup.

"Just put them in the sink," said Melissa as Reggie went to open the dishwasher. "It's your Dad's turn on Sundays." Melissa pointed at a chart on the fridge that definitely wasn't there yesterday.

We all squinted at it: 'Washing Up Rota'. My name was down for Thursdays.

"What's *that?*" I said.

"What do you think it is, dumbo?" asked Shannon.

"Well I know what it is, but why do we need one of those when we have a dishwasher?"

"We don't have a dishwasher, or at least we won't after today," said Dad, tidying up the table.

"You getting rid of yours too, Mr Batty?" asked Charlie, swiping a last piece of fruit.

"Makes sense," said Dad. "They cost a packet to run."

"That's rubbish," I said. "We did it last year in school.

You use less water and it hardly uses any electricity."

"My mum says they make you soft," called Charlie from the hall.

Dad turned to Melissa. "Help?"

"It's going, and that's that," she said, which didn't explain anything.

"You'll get used to it," Shannon added, who was perhaps the last person in the world I expected to agree.

And that seemed to be the end of the matter. Reggie, Shannon and Charlie disappeared into the lounge and I sat in silence with Dad and Melissa for as long as I could stand, which was about 30 seconds.

I grabbed my jacket from the hall and looked in on the others. All three were bent over the table; Shannon was folding, and the boys were colouring. I was about to leave them to it when I noticed: the TV had gone.

"The TV," I said, pointing unnecessarily. "What's happened to it?"

"Dunno," said Reggie, not looking up.

"They can't get rid of the telly!"

"What's the matter? Worried about missing your boring old wildlife documentaries?" said Shannon.

"But... don't you *care?*" Nobody looked up. "Are you going to go along with all this until there's nothing left?" No reaction.

"Pass me the red felt tip please, Charlie," Shannon said.

I left the room and slammed the door behind me. Bang! It sounded good. I'm sure I could hear the others laughing, so for good measure I did it again as I left the house. Bang!

Chapter 22
TIDDLES

"IT'S LIKE DAD doesn't want us to have any fun," I said to Izzy as she grabbed hold of me and we whizzed down the zipwire.

"It's not just you, you know," said Izzy as we climbed the fort. "Our telly has gone, too. Mum said there was nothing on, so we might as well put my chess table there instead."

I was distracted for a moment, thinking about how Izzy was the only person I know who would have her personal chess table.

"And what about Shannon?" I said, swinging from a monkey bar. "She's gone really weird."

"Teenagers do that," called Izzy from the top of the Witch's Hat. "Mum said so."

We flopped down on the bench, exhausted. "Well it doesn't make any sense, especially when your dad is going out with a spy. And now we can't get into Enid's house either, so there's nowhere to have a secret meeting."

The sound of an electric motor caught our attention: a white golf buggy was pulling up outside the park. I knew what was coming next. "Come on, let's get out of here."

"But we've only just arrived!" protested Izzy as I

grabbed her arm.

"Believe me, we don't want to stick around."

Kristi bounded out of the buggy like a puppy. "Hey girls!" she shouted.

"She's another nutter," I said under my breath, and we ran laughing out of the opposite gate.

"Don't look back, she'll kill you with her super smile," I panted.

"Girls! Girls!" Kristi shouted. "Girls! Hey, girls!" Kristi's voice faded away behind us as we sprinted down the road, towards the school.

Eventually we slowed to a walk, chatting in the sunshine.

"Look!" shouted Izzy. As we ran, a red paper plane was swooping down towards us, just out of reach.

I knew where that had come from. Squinting into the sun I could see Charlie and Reggie up on the rock behind the church, jumping up and down and waving their arms.

We ran along underneath the plane, elbowing each other out of the way as we tried to grab it. And then, as it came within reach, a gust of wind lifted it up and over the school gates.

Izzy and I watched as it glided down again, circling gently until it came to rest on the windscreen wiper of the only car to be seen on this Sunday afternoon – Mr Frost's bright, sunshine orange convertible.

We walked on and met the boys outside the churchyard. Shannon had apparently decided she couldn't be bothered to climb up to the rock and had gone off to meet her friends – that sounded more like her. Perhaps she was back to normal.

"Did you see that aeroplane go?" said Charlie as we walked back towards the house. "It shot off like a rocket!"

"I think an aeroplane that's like a rocket *is* a rocket," said Izzy.

"No, it was definitely an aeroplane," said Charlie.

"Who cares. I wonder what Mr Frost will say when he finds it," said Reggie, looking at Charlie. "He might guess who it's from."

"He'll probably chuck it," I said. "How could he know?"

"Maybe he'll recognise the handwriting?" said Reggie, raising one eyebrow. Charlie sniggered.

"Uh-oh. What have you done, boys?"

"Nothing!" said Charlie.

"We might have put a little message inside," said Reggie.

"We didn't know Frosty would get it!" laughed Charlie.

"What kind of little message?"

"Well... you tell them Charlie, it was your idea..."

"Yeah but you wrote it, I didn't know how to spell it."

"What on earth did you write?" asked Izzy.

"We wrote, "If you find this, you smell like a badger.'"

I laughed so hard I had to stop walking. Reggie and Charlie kept saying "What?", pretending they didn't know what they'd done, and Izzy stood there, tutting.

On the way home we passed the shop on the green. On the window was an intriguing sign:

The Bullies Have Won!
Confectionery Sale: Last Day
EVERYTHING REDUCED

"I'm surprised," said Izzy. "Mrs Levett doesn't like being told what to do."

I shrugged. "It looks like she's playing the game now, though."

"I'm going to see what's left," said Charlie, and bundled into the shop.

Ten minutes later he was out, clutching a carrier bag stuffed with crisps, chocolate and sweets.

"There was loads and it was really cheap. I spent all my money," he said. "She was dead grumpy about it, though." No change there then.

We had a peek inside Charlie's bag because we knew he'd be sharing them. Charlie always got more pocket money than the rest of us put together, but we couldn't be jealous because he gave away most of what he bought. "Why would I want to eat sweets on my own?" he often said.

By the time we got back to our house we were starving.

"Let's eat them next door," said Reggie.

"We can't," I said. "It's locked, remember? We'll have to eat them in our bedroom."

"Nah. We'll get Tiddles to open up," Reggie grinned.

Izzy and I looked at each other blankly. Charlie was chuckling.

"Who's Tiddles?" we said in unison.

Reggie pointed in Charlie's direction, but I couldn't see anyone or anything that might be called Tiddles.

"What are you talking about, Reggie?" This was quite annoying.

Reggie smiled.

"Miaow," said Charlie.

"Come on Tiddles, show them what you can do!" said Reggie, running off with Charlie.

Izzy and I shrugged and followed the giggling boys around the side of the house.

Sure enough the door was firmly locked: no amount of pushing and shoving would open it.

"Come on then, Charlie, you do it if you're so strong," I said, moving to one side.

"I'm Tiddles, remember?" said Charlie, taking his jumper off.

"Oh yeah, whatever," I said, watching as Charlie pulled open the Velcro straps on his shoes. "What *are* you doing, Charlie – sorry, Tiddles?"

"He's going to get us into the house," said Reggie. "Watch."

By now Charlie had taken off his trousers and his t-shirt, and was standing in his pants and socks.

"Ugh, gross," said Izzy. "Look at your tummy!"

It's true that Charlie did have quite a big tummy on him – round and white, like dough rising in a bowl. But if Charlie thought that was a rude thing to say – and it was – he certainly didn't show it.

"My tummy is brilliant," said Charlie, giving it a slap. "Why would you want a little one? Where would you put all your dinner?"

"Good point," I said.

"*And* it helps me get into small spaces," added Charlie, confusingly.

"Come on then Tiddles, let's get inside," said Reggie.

For the first time, I noticed that Enid's back door had a catflap – quite a big one, as catflaps go. I remembered that not long before Enid had moved out, a man had come round to fit a new one: Dudley was clearly getting too porky for the old one (if a cat can get porky).

But this flap certainly wasn't *that* big. It wasn't like a trap door or anything. But Charlie didn't seem in the slightest bit worried as he crouched down, reached through with one arm and pushed his head through.

"Is this a good idea?" Izzy asked Reggie. "What if he can't get out?"

"He'll be fine," said Reggie. "He did it last time."

"Why don't you do it? You're much skinnier," I said.

"Me? No chance," said Reggie. "What if I got stuck?"

There was no answer to that, and no way Charlie was going to fit. No way at all. He was now wriggling and twisting, kicking his legs into the air as if that would give him a push. To be fair, he soon managed to get his other arm through and then turned on his side, his head and shoulders inside the house and his big tummy definitely outside.

"How're you doing, Charlie?" shouted Reggie.

"Great!" came the muffled reply. "I don't think I'll need the cream cheese this time!"

Reggie explained. "Last time he got a bit stuck, so I got my sandwiches out of my lunchbox and smeared the slices all over his belly to make it slippy."

"And did that help?"

"Yeah! He was in big trouble when he got home, though. He told his Mum he'd slipped and fallen into his

150

sandwich. She sent him to bed early."

"He's crazy," muttered Izzy, and I had to agree.

"Right, ready now!" shouted Charlie, and Reggie crouched down behind him, one hand on each foot.

"After three! One, two, three, SUCK!"

On the word "suck", Reggie gave Charlie's feet an almighty shove while Charlie rippled his tummy in a most unusual way. It was like a wave of Play-Doh, starting near his pants and travelling up towards his neck.

"Again! One, two, three, SUCK!"

Over and over they did it, and to our amazement, inch by inch, Charlie's tummy inched its way through the catflap. Finally, he fell down inside the door with a thud, pulled his feet through, and opened the latch with a beaming smile.

"See! I couldn't do that if I didn't have a big tummy!"

Izzy and I couldn't argue with that kind of logic, so we didn't try. We were in.

Chapter 23
EMERGENCY MEETING

AFTER CHARLIE HAD shown off the red marks on his tummy and got dressed we sat in a circle on the floor, and he shared out the crisps and sweets.

"Right, I'm calling this an Emergency Meeting," I said.

"Emergency? What emergency?" asked Izzy.

"She means the sweet notice at the shop," said Charlie, tucking into my Cheese and Onion Spudders.

"Are you mad? Have you lot been asleep? About The Changes, of course! The bikes! The Reflection Room! The telly, and the internet, and the dishwasher, and –"

"OK OK," said Izzy, "we get you."

"But some of those things are –"

" –great, yes, I know that, Reggie." I said. This was *so* frustrating. "That's really not the point."

Reggie shrugged and popped in another Fizzy Finger. For a moment nobody spoke.

"So did you see Melissa go out spying again?" asked Izzy.

"Yes, I did," I said, "Really late. She's definitely up to something."

"Where does she go?" asked Charlie.

"I dunno. I fell asleep."

"Maybe she meets up with other spies?" said Reggie.

"I love pies," said Charlie, his mouth full of crisps. Sometimes I think he does it on purpose. We ignored him.

"But it has to be somewhere in the village," Izzy pointed out.

"Maybe not," said Reggie. "She's in one of those spy cars, remember. We don't know how fast it goes. She could go right into town, or outer space."

I sighed. I put my hands on the floor behind my head to make a crab, anything to stop myself going crazy. Now *that* was odd. Upside down, something about this room looked different, and I don't mean upside down different.

I turned the right way up and walked over to the locked stair door. On the wall next to it was a picture that definitely hadn't been there before: it was a poem, written in fancy writing. *Go placidly amid the noise and haste*, it began, before the text got smaller and too hard to read.

"That picture has moved!" said Reggie, pointing. I nodded, running my hands over a patch of light wallpaper near the front door. It was the same size as the framed poem.

I held my hand to the frame. It moved under my touch, so I gave it a sideways push and it swung easily on its nail. A flash of glossy black caught my eye so I pushed further to reveal a touch panel underneath – exactly the same as the ones on the bike racks.

I looked at the others and without waiting for their opinion, pressed my palm against it.

Access denied. This premises is protected with Dye Explosion Technology. You have TWO more attempts.

The woman's voice echoed round the room; nobody spoke. This definitely wasn't the friendly squawking parrot.

"Maybe my hand will open it," said Charlie. Before I could stop him he had pushed his sugary hand against the reader.

Access denied. You have ONE more attempt.

"Maybe my other hand," said Charlie.

"NO!" we all shouted as Charlie reached out. With a giant shove I sent Charlie pinballing across the room, crashing into Reggie before bouncing off onto the sofa.

"Thora! What're you doing, you idiot!" said Charlie, pulling himself to his feet and picking up his half-eaten crisps.

"Do you really think the spies are up there?" whispered Izzy.

"Well not right now," I said. "But where else would they go?"

The atmosphere had changed, now that we knew we were basically sitting underneath a spies' den.

"So what now?" said Reggie, looking to me. The others did the same, and I felt my stomach contract with the attention.

"I'm not sure," I muttered. "Here, give me your jumper." I took it across to the panel and rubbed at Charlie's sticky fingerprints before replacing the framed poem carefully.

"We need a plan," said Izzy.

"We need to find out what's upstairs, that's what we need to do," I said. "But we can't, so we're going to be stuck in this miserable village for the rest of our lives."

"I bet Melissa is the only one who can open it," said Izzy.

"Or maybe one of the others," said Reggie, "like the one with the big feet."

154

"Since we don't know who the others are, that doesn't help much."

"I know what we do!" said Charlie.

We all looked at Charlie. Finally, someone with a plan.

"We cut off Melissa's hand when she isn't looking, and use it to open the door." Charlie ripped open a bag of Jelly Toes with a grin on his face.

"I *think* she might notice that," said Reggie, squashing and rolling a Jelly Toe between his fingers like a giant bogey. Disgusting boy.

"So what now?" Izzy asked me, as if I was her Mum.

"Well... " I said. I'd done that thing where you start the sentence, hoping that by the time you're half-way through you'll have a good idea how to end it. I didn't. "I dunno. Maybe we just keep watching Melissa. She's bound to make a mistake sometimes, spies always do."

They all nodded although I doubt if anyone understood, including me. It didn't seem like much of a plan. We didn't even know which side she was on.

"One thing's for sure," said Reggie, looking out of the window. "We definitely don't want to be here when Melissa gets back. Like, in two minutes."

Outside, Melissa was climbing out of a familiar bright orange sports car.

You've never seen us move so fast: we scooped up all the remaining packets of sweets into the bag, ran for the door and were out into the garden in seconds. We crawled through Enid's hedge out into the side passage, checked to see if Frosty had left, and then casually wandered out into the cul-de-sac. It was an Oscar-winning performance, there's no way anyone could have known.

Izzy and Charlie peeled off home for tea, and Reggie and I piled through the front door with a very cheery, super-loud "Hello!"

Melissa called out from the kitchen. "Had a good day, guys?" she said, smiling.

"Yeah," we said. But did *you* have a good day, I thought? Spy anything interesting?

"Because I've got a very good idea what you've been up to," she continued.

My heart nearly stopped. My fingers felt clammy. I thought I needed a sit down. I had grabbed the bag of sweets as we left, and I passed it to Reggie behind his back.

"Oh yeah?" he said, bending down to take off his shoes and pushing the bag behind the shoe rack, cool as a cucumber.

"Yep," she said, meeting us in the hall. Reggie looked up as Melissa pulled her hand from behind her back. She was holding a crumpled red paper aeroplane.

"Ah!" we both shouted. The relief I felt was so great it almost made the heart attack worth it. But then we knew where she'd found that paper plane – on Frosty's car. And what would she be doing with him? Because there's no way that Frosty was on our side, and Frosty's new friend was Mr Wharton. And who did Mr Wharton count as his friends?

As Reggie disappeared into the kitchen to find out what was for tea, I couldn't help thinking that maybe Melissa wasn't such a smart cookie after all. She'd made a mistake already, like I predicted. Maybe we could outsmart her, get to the bottom of The Changes. The big question now though: could we outsmart *everyone?*

Chapter 24
ROAD CLOSED

A FEW DAYS later, Reggie and I took a couple of Village Bikes out after school to explore. Starting in the play park we meandered towards the village green; a steady stream of mums and dads trudged towards us, peeling off to their different streets and houses. You could occasionally see the bright purple of a factory sweatshirt, or a white collar peeking out from under their heavy coats and scarves. Everyone looked pretty grumpy.

When we reached the green I raced Reggie, trying to lap him. But in recent months he had become much quicker, and it seemed more likely Reggie would lap me instead. Our shouts across the empty green were swallowed up, like a toddler jumping into a ball pit.

"Hey, Thora! Where are all the cars?" Reggie yelled breathlessly, only one corner behind me.

He was right: there were normally a few on the road, or even parked up on the green itself. When that happened, Mrs Levett – the woman from the shop with a famously short temper – would stomp across in her apron to harangue the driver, or slip a photocopied note under their windscreen if they weren't around. The note instructed them in red ink to 'get your dirty car off our village green'.

But today Reggie was right: no cars and just the odd tyre track. There weren't any on the side roads I could see, either. And that was definitely strange, because it was about the time that everyone arrived home from work and we had our village version of a traffic jam – the same as a normal one, but over in about five minutes.

On the next circuit I led Reggie back down the main road that headed up from the valley. "Let's see where everyone is coming from."

Five minutes later we'd reached the edge of the village. The new bike rack, installed on the site of the old dairy car park, was virtually full. The dairy itself closed before I was born and was boarded up, but the car park was still used occasionally by walkers, and even once by a travelling fair.

But today this scruffy patch of gravel was transformed, packed with row upon row of cars. Reggie and I leaned on our handlebars, watching vehicles zig zag slowly up and down, looking for a space. Others had parked up wherever they could on the verges, and a last few drivers were locking up and setting off for home.

"Well that's one mystery solved at least," I said. "Except I still don't know why they don't drive into the village."

At that moment Charlie's dad appeared. "Hello kids," he said, pulling on his rucksack.

"Hello Mr Barnes," said Reggie. "Why aren't you parking in the village any more?"

"Because I don't have a tank to drive over *those*," he smiled, pointing towards two new signs and some kind of speed bump that had been installed just past the entrance to the carpark. "See you around kids. Have fun!"

Fun? I don't think I even knew what fun was any more.

Although if I had my own tank, that would *definitely* be fun.

We cycled over. It was no ordinary speed bump: rows of sharp, pointed metal teeth were embedded into the road, ready to chew up anything or anyone that tried to drive into the village.

Next to the teeth was one of the familiar hand sensors on a post. Reggie wheeled up and tried it. "Access Denied," purred the American voice.

"Hey, look," said Reggie, pointing up at a sign. In too-big-to-miss red letters, it said:

"Village closed to motor traffic. FF restrictions apply."

"I wonder why they've done that?" I scratched my head. "At least we know why Pizza Presto won't deliver."

"And why Roberto hasn't been up yet," added Reggie.

Roberto was our friendly ice cream man. You knew spring was on the way as soon as you heard the chimes of his van grinding its way into the village, black smoke streaming from the exhaust. He would park up on the green and Mrs Levett would storm out and hand him a rude note, of course. So he'd blow kisses at her retreating back and then sell us ice creams as big as our head. But so far this year, no sign.

Everything past the road closure looked normal: fields, sheep and the occasional tractor.

"Let's go home," I said.

"Do we have to?" said Reggie. "There's nothing to do, nothing to watch, and nothing I want to eat."

I nodded. "I'm not keen either. But yeah, we have to."

We turned around. I hadn't realised how much height we'd lost already so we were soon huffing and puffing, weaving all over the road. I was slightly ahead when I heard Reggie shout out, and his bike clatter to the ground.

I looked back: Reggie was sprawled in the middle of the road, untangling himself from his bike and rubbing his elbow. Behind him, bumper almost over Reggie's back wheel, was a white golf buggy. And emerging from the door, limb by gangly limb, was Mr Wharton.

"Goodness, boy, what's the matter with you?" he said, striding over.

"I didn't even know you were there!" said Reggie. "You drove up behind me and frightened me off my bike!"

"No, no, no, you're quite incorrect," said Mr Wharton. "You stopped right in front of me, I had absolutely no choice." He looked at me as if wanting my support, which he certainly wasn't going to get.

"You OK Reggie? Want me to fetch Dad?"

"Nah, I'm OK," he said, pulling his bike upright and inspecting his grazed arm.

"Well, no harm done," said Mr Wharton, before turning back towards his buggy. "Hey. Hey! Stop! My buggy! Hey!" he shouted.

The empty buggy was slowly starting to roll back down the hill. Mr Wharton broke into a trot, and then a sprint.

"Hey! Hey! PUT THE BRAKE ON!"

And to our amazement, it stopped. Just like that.

Reggie and I looked at each other. "That's not possible. Cars can't stop themselves like that."

"They can if someone does it for you," I said. "Look, there's someone else in there."

Sure enough, in the front bench seat we could see the top of someone's head, black hair bobbing. I wasn't sure who it was, but Reggie recognised her immediately.

"Melissa! Hey, Melissa!"

The head froze for a second, before Melissa's face appeared with a sheepish smile. She looked like she'd been caught eating someone else's sweets.

"Oh, hi there kids," she said, reluctantly getting out of the buggy. "Geoff – err, Mr Wharton was giving me a lift home. Very kind of him."

I wondered where Melissa had been to need a lift home – or Mr Wharton, for that matter; I hadn't seen any golf buggies in the car park. And another thing: it wasn't Melissa's home.

"Well you won't be able to get home, not now," said Reggie. "It's all closed off."

"Don't you worry about us. Well, glad to know you're tickety-boo young Reginald," said Mr Wharton. "See you later, and – "

"...have fun," I muttered under my breath. Not likely, I thought as he steered his way around us and they headed up the hill, Melissa giving us both a small, awkward wave.

"Why do they keep telling us to have fun when they're making it impossible?" Reggie asked.

"Someone, somewhere, is determined to make us miserable," I said. "I'm pretty sure I know who. I just don't know why.'

Chapter 25
DAD'S DINNER

I SAT AT the kitchen table with my homework while Dad prepared dinner. Homework was taking longer and longer these days; not only because I had more to do, but because there wasn't a reason to rush through and finish. It lasted for hours.

There was more bad news: now that Dad wasn't allowed to bring home Tommy Thumb's Big Beef Pie or a Monster Meat Mashup, he was cooking more instead. And if it wasn't pancakes or eggy bread, Dad didn't really have a clue. And to make matters worse, he thought he was quite good.

With Melissa we got a salad, fish, couscous, or wholewheat pasta. Nothing to make you whoop with joy, but you could eat it. But Dad preferred to take a different approach, one that he said "brought out the flavour."

It wasn't a quick process, mind you. This particular effort had begun the previous evening when he hacked some vegetables into chunks and pushed them around a frying pan before adding anything he could find. Lumps of gristly meat, stringy celery that he'd forgotten to put in earlier, flour and stock cubes. And then for his signature flourish, he dumped in tablespoons of dusty mixed herbs from a big sack he'd found at the back of the cupboard.

"Rosie and I brought it back from somewhere," he had commented, giving it a sniff. That made it at least five years old. "Smells of holidays, lasts forever."

It all went into a casserole dish along with a kettle full of water and two mugs of lentils. And then he slammed it into the oven that morning to simmer all day long, filling the house with a vile, sweet-sour pong.

"Almost ready," he said, dumping cutlery onto the table. Just need glasses –"

He was interrupted by the shatter of a glass slipping off the draining board, shards scattering across the kitchen. I tucked my feet under my bottom without a word. Dad sighed heavily, threw the teatowel over his shoulder, and fetched the broom.

"Yuck," he said as he swept the space under the counter where the dishwasher had been. It was now sitting outside the back door, grubby and unloved. I looked up as he hooked out piles of brown gunk, an action figure, a teaspoon and 20p.

"See, you're saving money already, Dad," I said. He looked at me and raised his eyebrow.

Enough was enough. Time to unravel this mystery by turning to the only grown-up I still trusted. "Dad, I have a question, but you have to tell me the truth. Promise?"

Dad stood up, and leaned on his broom for a moment. Then he glanced at the sensor in the corner, reached over and turned on the radio. We didn't have it on so much now, as it had developed an irritating habit of cutting out, especially during the news. On the plus side, this meant we hardly ever heard the Prime Minister banging on about his revolutionary ideas any more. Dad twiddled the knob until pop music came on, and turned it up loud. Very loud.

Sitting down at the table, he leaned in towards us. "Promise," he mouthed, his face deadly serious.

Right, truth time. "Dad. Is Melissa a secret agent?"

A broad smile spread across Dad's face and he threw his head back, laughing.

Dad put his face right up against mine. "I'm afraid not," he said. "She works for the Department of Education and Social Affairs, doing a job so dull I fall asleep every time she talks about it."

"It's just... you know... The changes... " I ground to a halt. I hadn't thought this through. What could I say? She goes out at night sometimes? She asks a lot of questions? She likes vegetables? Not exactly smoking guns, were they? And I could hardly say we'd been poking around at Enid's house and noticed a handprint scanner and nearly blew the place up.

"So what about you?" I asked.

"Me? A secret agent? Well. That's a different matter. I might be," said Dad.

My heart started pounding. "Really?"

"It's definitely possible. But then if I was, I couldn't tell you, could I? So you'll never know."

"But... you promised!"

"Secret agents' promises are different," said Dad. "They get paid to fib. Right, I need to get this dinner on the table before you torture the truth out of me."

Melissa pushed her plate forward. "I'm not hungry," she said. "I had a big lunch. But you guys eat all of yours."

For once, all of us were eating dinner together. Or more accurately, *not* eating dinner. The huge dish of steaming hotpot squatted in the middle of the table, impossible to ignore. Grey-brown lumps lurked in a glutinous paste, peppered through with white balls that were sometimes fat, sometimes uncooked flour. The dry and lumpy mash wasn't much better; it refused to mix with the car-crash stew so each mouthful was doubly disgusting.

Everyone had been sitting in near silence, just the sound of forks scraping as we pushed the pieces of dried up pork around the plate. Even Shannon's chit-chat had dried up.

"I'm not hungry either," said Reggie, copying Melissa.

"Nor me," I said, pushing my plate forward at the same time as Shannon.

"I'm not so peckish either, now you mention it," said Dad.

Melissa half-smiled. "It wasn't your best, John."

"It was like lumpy pig glue," said Reggie. "Horrible."

"Come on. I wouldn't say *horrible*," said Melissa.

"I would," said Dad.

"Revolting," said Reggie.

"Gross," said Shannon.

"Sickening," added Reggie.

"Properly nauseating," I said.

"Not quite sure what went wrong there," said Dad, clipping me around the ear and standing up to clear our plates. "It looked so delicious when I was making it."

"You tried your best," said Melissa, clearing our plates. "Right, let's all have some pudding." She looked around for ideas. "Fruit?" she said hopefully, offering a hand of bananas. Disappointing. Fruit is OK, but I like a pudding you can stick a chocolate flake in.

We took one reluctantly.

"Thanks," said Shannon cheerily. "I love bananas."

It was news to me that Shannon loved anything inside these four walls, but Brand New Shannon was clearly here to stay. She was like a bad actor in a play, slapping me and Reggie on the back or lifting up her eyebrows and smiling at us, even though there was no reason.

And another thing. Shannon's taste in make-up until now had always been bold. Big eyeshadow. Painted eyebrows. Purple lipstick. But since her 18th birthday, she'd gone natural. The make-up had vanished: if she was wearing any, I couldn't tell. And her hair was now smooth and glossy, swinging like a shiny curtain as she did big laughs at unfunny stuff.

Shannon wolfed down her banana and with a glance at the kitchen clock, got to her feet. "Right, I've got to go," she said breezily.

"What, now?" I said.

"Yep," she said. "Need to borrow something from a friend."

"At this time?" I asked.

"Yes! You have to remember, I'm 18 now. I can come and go as I like." She sounded very pleased with herself.

"I'm going to pop out and sort a few things too if that's OK," said Melissa to Dad, who nodded.

"Can I go out too?" said Reggie.

"Nope," said Melissa, putting her plate in the sink.

"You and Thora should play Chinese Checkers," said

Shannon from the door.

"You're funny," said Reggie.

"Chess?"

"Dull," I said.

"Colour in some pictures, then? What about a game – dressing up?"

Reggie looked at her witheringly, as if she'd suggested he needed his nappy changing.

"Still, you two have fun. Why don't you have a play in the lounge before bed? Or you could maybe have a chat about stuff."

"What stuff?" asked Reggie.

"Oh I don't know," said Shannon, suddenly sounding vague. "You know, stuff you're thinking."

"Shannon," Melissa said in a warning tone. It seemed that Melissa was now allowed to tell Shannon off. Interesting.

"Yeah, right. Thanks for that idea," I said. "I'll file it under 'useless'."

That kind of backchat would have earned me a slap or a scream in the old days, but that night she just smiled at me. "Please yourself," she said, before doing something extraordinary: she leaned in and gave us both a kiss. I could not remember her ever doing that before.

"Bleurgh," said Reggie, pulling away.

"Come on, let's get you on your way," said Melissa, holding open the kitchen door.

"See you in a bit!" Shannon said merrily and then they was gone, out of the front door with a happy slam. Reggie and I looked at each other quizzically, and then at Dad. But Dad was suddenly very busy with the washing up.

Chapter 26
THE BIG PRETEND

WE GOT NO further forward with Dad. He stonewalled our questions, saying he hadn't a clue where they'd gone, and it was none of our business anyway.

As I plodded upstairs a little while later I spotted the carrier bag of sweets, still hidden behind the shoe rack. We hadn't been back to Enid's since: what would be the point? A spy might turn up at any moment, and we couldn't get past the handprint scanner to investigate. I looked inside and ate one of the Jelly Toes out of the half-opened packet – hopefully not one that Reggie had been squishing like modelling clay.

I stopped dead on the stairs, struck by an idea. A Big Idea.

"Reggie! Reggie!" I called, bursting into our bedroom. "Where's your Play Pack?"

"Dunno," said Reggie, who was trying to stack up draughts counters as high as he could. "Under the bed, maybe?"

I fished out his brown envelope and tipped the contents onto Reggie's bed.

"Hey! That's mine!"

"Forget about that. I know how to get past the scanner

at Enid's. I need your Plasticine."

"What about yours?" he protested.

"Yep, I need that too," I said, fetching it out of my bedside drawer and replacing it with the sweets. "Right, come with me. And don't say a word."

Downstairs, Reggie followed me into the kitchen where Dad was washing up.

"Do we have a big baking tray or something, Dad?"

"I thought you were off to bed, but sure," he said, passing one from the cupboard.

"And a rolling pin?"

"Yep, that too." He passed one across, and tilted his head to one side. "What are you two trouble-makers up to?"

"Homework," I said. "Nearly forgot. We're doing a project at school, about Famous People."

"I thought you were doing The Tudors?" said Reggie.

"No, that's next week," I said, kicking him hard and making a face.

"And you need the baking tray for what, exactly?" Dad asked, puzzled.

"You'll see. Here, Reggie, you can help too. Roll your pack into squares," I said. I took a pickle jar from the recycling so I could roll my pack at the same time.

"How big?" asked Reggie.

"About as big as..." I tried to think of something the right size, "...a book."

We rolled and patted until we each had four squares which I carefully transferred to the baking tray in a chequerboard pattern, watched by a curious Dad.

"OK, so now what?" said Reggie.

"We're nearly done. All we need now –"

I was interrupted by the sound of voices.

"Hey look, Melissa's back already," said Dad. "And Shannon too, double the fun."

The pair burst through the front door, laughing about something as if they were sisters.

"You should have seen them, it was hilarious!" screeched Shannon as they came into the kitchen. She took a carrot from the fridge and started eating it noisily, smacking her lips and saying "yum" a lot. Back to the bad acting.

"Hey, what's with the crafty stuff? Well done, guys! What is it?"

"It's famous people homework," I said, gritting my teeth. "I'll give you a clue. Hollywood?"

"Nope," said Shannon, crunching away. "No idea."

"I do," said Melissa, smiling. Butterflies danced in my tummy; this could be about to go horribly wrong. "You've made the Walk of Fame, haven't you? Where all those movie stars get their photos taken?"

"Yes!" I said with a relieved smile. "So Reggie, press your hand into this square and I'll write your name underneath."

I grabbed Reggie's wrist and pressed it in; not bad, a bit squidgy but it was only a practice.

"Right, they all have to be different to look good, so I'll have a go..." I said. That was much better. A nice crisp outline of my hand. "OK. That works." I pretended to admire my homework. "Who's up next? Melissa and Shannon, can you help?"

Shannon was straight over, flicking her hair, taking

pretend selfies and acting like she was a movie star. Dad was next, then Melissa.

"Just one slot left." I pretended to scratch my head. "Melissa, do your other hand, just so it looks different."

"Rightio. All sorted?" asked Dad.

"Yep," I said, admiring our handiwork.

"Right, off to bed, the pair of you."

"Night, Dad!" I shouted, carrying my tray carefully up the stairs.

We lay on our beds and read. It wasn't massively comfy because our lovely soft duvets had been replaced by sheets and scratchy woollen blankets. Dad had said they were better for you, but when we asked he why laughed and said because somebody said so. It didn't seem very funny in the middle of the night when the sheets were all wrapped around your legs and the blanket had slipped onto the floor.

I tried to read again, but I didn't last long. I sighed, and shuffled, and coughed a bit but I couldn't get Reggie's attention. He lay on his back with his knees in the air, reading Harry Potter between his legs. It looked extremely uncomfortable, but it didn't seem to bother him.

It was getting late, and dark. Dad had gone out for a run; that's how keen he was these days, running into the night. I went downstairs for a glass of water, more for something to do than anything else. The lights were off except in the kitchen where I could hear Melissa tap-tapping on her laptop.

She was facing away from me as I entered, her computer

screen filled with numbers, as usual.

"Hi Melissa."

I saw her shoulders tense, and she moved her left hand suddenly. I heard a rustling noise.

"What're you doing?" I asked, walking round. Melissa had her head down, long hair hanging over her face.

"Fnuffng," she mumbled.

"Hey, what's *that?*" I said, pointing at the corner of a shiny blue wrapper that was poking out from underneath her laptop. She put her hand over it. "Is that a Toffee Tangle wrapper?"

Melissa looked up, through her hair. There was a twinkle in her blue-green eyes and a bulge in her cheek.

"May-gee," she said, through her chewy mouthful.

"WHAT?! How come you –"

Melissa was out of her seat in a flash before I could shout the house down and put her finger on my lips. "Not a word," she whispered, before taking my hand.

"Hang on. Look the other way for a second," she said.

And so I did: straight out of the kitchen window… at a perfect reflection of the room. Behind me, Melissa clambered up onto the worktop and reached behind the camera before jumping down, stealthy as a cat.

"Right, we're good." She led me over to the boiler cupboard, reached up on tiptoes and fished out another familiar blue packet. "I'll share my emergency supplies with you," she said. "Just this once."

We sat at the table in silence. The toffees were soft from the heat of the boiler; the tangles had collapsed, and I used my teeth to scrape them out of the wrapper.

"That was delicious," I said, as Melissa typed away.

"Can I have some more?"

"You ate my last one," she said without looking up.

"Maybe Dad has some more."

"No." Melissa's voice suddenly had a sharp edge. She looked hard at me. "That was a little slip. The last of the bad stuff." Her voice softened. "I'll do more cooking," she said. "I'll make sure your Dad doesn't make any more hotpots." She grinned.

"They're worse than the new school dinners, and that's saying something," I said.

"They don't seem to be doing you any harm. You're doing really well," said Melissa. "Great result in your maths test last week, and your spellings are better now, too."

I frowned. "How do you know that?" I looked at Melissa's laptop. In a smooth, swift movement she closed the lid.

"Have you got that on your computer?"

"What? No," said Melissa. "I... I bumped into Mrs Scott in the shop. Anyway, if you go on like this you'll find high school a breeze."

"Yeah, I guess so." I wondered whether Mrs Scott told everyone about our test results in the shop.

"Mrs Scott said you haven't used the Reflection Room for a while?"

"Nobody does," I said. "Reggie says – " but I stopped.

Melissa was looking at me. "Yes? What does Reggie say?"

"Oh, nothing. Doesn't matter."

"You know it takes a while to get used to new things, don't you, Thora? What seems unusual now soon becomes normal. And then you start to realise why it's better."

I didn't say anything. This sounded like code to me. I wished Izzy was there to help me work it out.

"It may take a while, but you'll realise someday that these days are... well, they really are the best days of your life. And you're right in the middle of some very exciting times."

OK, this was definitely code. "Exciting" was the last word I'd use to describe life.

At that moment we heard the front gate clink; Dad was back.

"Quick, upstairs, before your Dad comes in. And remember," said Melissa, shoving a wrapper into her pocket, "not a word. Wouldn't want Dad thinking we didn't like his hotpot."

"OK, night night," I said. Melissa pulled me close for an awkward kiss-cuddle.

I padded out into the hall before stopping. There was no way Melissa could stop me saying goodnight to my Dad, so I closed the kitchen door, sat on the bottom step in the gloom and waited.

"Hello, piggles," said Dad when he flicked on the light switch and saw me. "I thought you'd be in bed." Dad slipped off his trainers and sat down next to me.

"Not quite. Just going."

I reached over and patted his belly. "It's definitely getting smaller," I said. "It's like someone is letting the air out of a space hopper. You smell sweaty though."

"Ah Thora. What you give with one hand, you take with the other." He leaned in and gave me a kiss.

He frowned. "You smell... nice. Sweet."

I said nothing.

"Right, be gone," he said, giving me a push up the stairs. "I need a drink."

"And a shower," I said.

He stuck out his tongue, hauled himself to his feet using the banister and opened the kitchen door. "Honey! I'm home!" he said, and pulled the door shut behind him.

Chapter 27
MIDNIGHT MISSION

BUT I DIDN'T go upstairs. I didn't go anywhere. I know it's wrong to eavesdrop, but Melissa had been trying to tell me something and I wanted to work out what it was.

So I sat there in the dark, knees to my chin, listening.

For a few minutes I could hear Dad filling his glass, and talking about his day. He'd had problems with one of the production lines; he'd spotted one of Ed's sheep loose down by the gully on the cycle back; the village car park was overflowing and they'd need to do something about it.

I was about to give up when it got interesting.

"I think Thora might still have some sweets knocking around," said Dad. "I could smell them on her."

"Ah yes," said Melissa. "That might be my fault."

"Oh?" said Dad, burping.

"She caught me with a Toffee Tangle just now."

"Ah come on Melissa, that's not on. We'll get fined, for starters. And they're not good for her."

"Oo, listen to you," said Melissa. "Mr Converted. And we won't be fined, I put the camera on Privacy Mode."

"Hang on – I thought your phone was in lockdown?"

"It is. There's an override switch at the back of the cameras."

176

"Well that's one good thing," said Dad. "I'm counting on this week's money. I've almost saved enough for the en suite bathroom."

"Viewing figures are up again," he said. "Biggest audience yet at the weekend, Shannon told me. Of course she thinks it's all her work."

"She would," said Melissa.

Viewing figures? Shannon? Audience? It was all so confusing I could scream.

"The school data looks good, too," said Melissa. "Up across the board – all subjects and aerobic fitness, too. I... "

"What?" said Dad, through a mouthful of something. Probably banana.

"I don't know," said Melissa. "I can't help thinking we're seeing what we want to see. It's not as if the kids are radiating happiness, is it?"

"That's quite a change of heart from you, isn't it? And anyway, I wouldn't know," said Dad. "I barely see them, they're always out and about. Which is a *good thing*, I should say."

"I see more of them than you do," she said. "And remember, there's always the break clause, if we need it."

"No way," said Dad. "We've been through this. We'd have to give back, what, half of the fee?"

Melissa murmured her agreement.

"And then you've still got to find somewhere else to live until the end of the trial. No way. We're in this until the end. I'm surprised you're talking that way, to be honest."

There was a silence.

"You're right," said Melissa. "It's been a long day. And I think Thora knows more than we think. We need to keep

177

an eye on her."

"Oh I doubt it," said Dad. "I didn't tell her anything when she was asking about you and Shannon earlier, and she's a happy-go-lucky sort. Are you heading out?

"Yes," said Melissa. "I'll just check in, make sure everything's set up. Won't be long."

"OK, see you in bed. I need a bath."

I was up the stairs and into the bedroom in seconds. I stared at the ceiling in the dark, thinking, listening to Reggie's breathing. From outside the familiar whining sound faded in and out, like a mosquito. I peered into the gloom and as expected the grey, moonlit streets were empty of people and cars: just charcoal shadows, smears of black and an occasional puddle of light from a kitchen window. I climbed back into bed.

Melissa was right about one thing: I did know more than she thought. None of it made any sense. But I knew where we *would* find the answers. I set my alarm clock and closed my eyes.

I was on a roller-coaster, looping up and down and round and round. But the coaster was getting rougher and rougher, jiggling me this way and that until I thought I was going to fall out. Bells were ringing and the crowd below was chanting my name: "Thora! Thora!"

I woke with a start, opening my eyes to see Reggie's face in the gloom. He was shaking me hard by the shoulder. "Thora! Thora! Your alarm clock!"

The clock had somehow slipped down the side of my

bed. I shook myself awake and fished it out.

"Hey, Reggie!" I whispered. He stopped, halfway back into bed. "Where are you going? Come on, I need your help!"

I pulled the bag of sweets out of my drawer, pushed it up my nightie and led Reggie downstairs to the kitchen, feeling my way. Closing the door, I worked my way around the worktop until I reached the corner. "Hold this," I whispered directly into Reggie's ear, pushing the bag into his arms. I could feel him trembling.

I climbed up and reached up towards the ceiling in the pitch dark, working my hands up the wall. At first I thought I might have got confused but then my hands found it: a plastic sphere. I allowed my fingers to creep around it: there, I'd found it. At the back, right by the wall bracket: a small switch that slid sideways with a click.

"Right," I said quietly, dropping to the floor and turning on the light over the hob. I tipped the contents of the bag over the table. "I need all the Jelly Toes we've got."

Following my lead, Reggie sorted the packets of hands and tipped them into the saucepan. I reckon we had about 100 – I had no idea if that was enough, but we'd soon see.

Turning the heat to low, I handed a wooden spoon to the bleary-eyed Reggie. "Keep stirring them. I'll be back in a minute."

By the time I returned with the tray of Plasticine the Jelly Toes were melting into each other, colours spiralling into rainbow whirlpools.

"Thora – what're we doing?" he whispered.

"It's like something I saw on YouTube once. Right, looking good," I said, taking the pan from Reggie.

As steadily as I could I poured the molten sweet mixture – now a murky brown colour – into a handprint that had an "M" scratched in the corner. You could feel the heat rising from the liquid, and the metal tray started warming up. There was enough to fill four hands, in the end: both of Melissa's, and then mine and Dad's.

I washed up the pan carefully and stuffed the empty wrappers into Reggie's pyjama trouser pockets as he waited patiently. The jelly tray had now cooled enough to hold, but the contents still shimmered and wobbled with every touch. I threw a tea towel over it: that would have to do.

"You get the door and the lights," I said, jumping up onto the work surface and flicking the switch on the camera. With Reggie ahead, I carried the tray upstairs like an unexploded bomb. In the grey light of the early morning I slid the tray onto the sill outside my bedroom window, shut the curtains and flopped back into bed.

Chapter 28
UP THE STAIRS

NEXT DAY AFTER school, the four of us stood in Enid's front room in front of the poem on the wall. The last rays of the sun were dancing on the ceiling; we'd had to wait for ages for Izzy. "I couldn't get away. I tried the Sicilian Defence, but Mum came back with the Yugoslav Attack," she had explained.

"Chess," I mouthed to Reggie and Charlie, who was wriggling back into his t-shirt. He'd done his catflap thing again to get us in.

I pulled my 'school project' out of a white carrier bag and gently peeled Melissa's jelly hand, complete with jelly fingerprints, out of the Plasticine mould. I swung the picture frame to one side.

"So then," I said, "who wants to do it?"

Reggie took Melissa's hand but as he was about to place it on the sensor, he gave it back to me.

"It's your idea, Thora, you do it."

I took a deep breath and raised it up.

"Wait!" said Izzy. "What if there's someone up there?"

I hadn't thought of that.

"Like who?" said Reggie, though he sounded a bit nervous.

"I dunno," said Izzy. "One of the spies, I guess."

We were all silent. There were a few distant cries from the play park, but nothing more.

"It'll be fine," I said.

"I'm not sure," said Izzy, but it was too late: I slapped the floppy brown hand onto the sensor, squidging each finger onto the glass.

With a mechanical click, the old lounge door – the one that looked like it hadn't opened in a decade – clicked open.

"Welcome Agent 462," said the silky voice.

We looked at each other and a shiver passed amongst us.

Through the door, stairs rose up to the landing. We could see the same well-worn flowery yellow carpet and tatty woodchip wallpaper as downstairs, but we could also hear a distinct electrical hum. We could almost smell the technology.

Reggie hesitated. As the eldest in the room, it was time for Thora Batty to take the lead.

I flicked the light switch but nothing happened. I probably would have stopped right there, but the others were pressed up behind me. So we stumbled up into the gloom with just the dim light from the lounge to guide us.

The stairs creaked like you'd expect old stairs to do. When I reached the landing I stopped and everyone else bumped into me like an episode of Scooby Doo, pushing me forward.

"Oi!"

"Shh!" said Izzy.

"Nah, there's nobody here," said Charlie. "At the moment, anyway. Come on, Reggie, let's explore."

Three rooms led off the landing, all with doors ajar. Taped to the cracked, yellowing paintwork were handwritten signs. To our left, *Studio*. The room was dark. Straight ahead was *Gallery*, and a faint, green glowing light was visible through the crack. And to the right, a sign saying *The Panopticon* with a smiley face drawn underneath it. From that door a flickering white light shone out across the landing.

I hesitated. Reggie pushed past me and headed for the door to the Studio. He pushed it open with the toe of his shoe, as if he expected to be greeted with wild dogs or something. Izzy and I headed for the Gallery. But our first view on entering was in fact of Reggie because the whole of one wall was a tinted glass panel, looking directly into the Studio. Reggie flicked an oversized light switch and bright lights flooded the room. The Studio had obviously been one of the bigger bedrooms but it had been completely transformed. The walls were painted in bright blues and greens with smooth black tiles on the floor. Against one side of the room were two bright orange sofas positioned in a 'v' shape with a glass coffee table between them. On the wall behind the sofas was a stencil of a huge, white, and very familiar FF logo. And above it, neon pink letters spelled out *The Fun Factor*.

Facing the sofas were two enormous TV cameras mounted on wheels, one in each corner.

Charlie pushed past Reggie and threw himself onto one of the orange sofas. "I'm on the telly!" he shouted, making faces at the cameras and jumping up and down like a monkey. Reggie joined him for a wrestle; it must be something about sofas that makes boys do that.

183

I stood rooted to the spot, trying to make sense of it all. Without warning a deep, booming voice filled the Studio: "Boys, stop mucking around!"

We all jumped. Reggie looked up in surprise, overbalanced and fell off the sofa, dragging Charlie after him.

"Boys, behave or I'm sending you to Frosty!"

The deep voice that rumbled from speakers near the ceiling cracked, and was followed by a giggle. I looked to my left where Izzy had her finger on a microphone, grinning. The Gallery was much smaller – a single bedroom at best. The floorboards were bare; you could still see remnants of pink wallpaper near the ceiling and the old window was boarded up. A desk ran along one wall with three chairs on castors. A box sat in the corner; *Spare WiFi Cameras* had been scrawled on the lid. I took a peek inside, but the sight of dozens of disconnected grey cameras like a haul of eyeballs gave me the creeps. I shut it again quickly.

Izzy plonked herself down in the middle. Through a big pane of glass we could see the boys, up to their tricks again on the sofas.

"Look," said Izzy, "it's a one-way mirror. And you can give the boys the willies doing this." She pressed a button on the base of the microphone and made ghost noises, but the boys in the Studio had worked us out and took no notice.

I flopped down into a chair and span around. An A4 sheet was tacked to the wall: "Fun Factor: audience figures (provisional)'. I peered at the bar chart underneath, trying to make sense of it. But there was a quicker way.

"Izzy, help me out. What does this mean?"

Izzy saw the chart, and smiled as you'd greet a long lost friend.

"So it's showing the audience figures for a programme called *The Fun Factor* since the start of the series," she said. "It looks like it's on every day, at 7.30 Monday to Friday, then at 6.30 on the weekends."

I nodded. That made sense: the only thing you could watch at that time on any channel was a nature documentary. We hadn't noticed it until one day a sports commentator was cut off mid-race and replaced by a blue whale.

"And then... wow, there's a lot of people watching. About 12 million for the launch, then 8 million viewers in the first week and now" – Izzy traced her finger across to the Y axis to make sure – "it's up to about 23 million."

Twenty-three million? That was half the country!

"What's Shannon got to do with this?" asked Izzy.

"What do you mean?"

"Someone's written her name on it, about two weeks ago. Just before the figures jumped up."

I shrugged. One mystery at a time, I thought.

I turned my attention to the switches and sliders. They were all labelled, but few of the labels made much sense. The power button was obvious enough; a red light and a soft hum announced that it was working. I tried one of the sliders to see what it felt like; white noise gradually filled the room, like a swarm of bees. Not very nice. I tried another and was unnerved by the sound of people laughing hysterically, on and on without tiring. Louder and louder they got as I moved the slider upwards, until it sounded like we were living in my worst nightmare.

"Turn it off!" yelled Izzy, pressing her hands against

her ears, and I pushed the slider back down to zero and pressed the Power button.

Also on the desk was a tatty red lever-arch folder. It was labelled with a hand-drawn FF logo, and a scrawled title: *Fun Factor Series Playbook*.

I flicked through: there were dozens of see-through plastic folders. The first was labelled Launch Week. Inside I could see scribbled notes and photos. I pulled out the photos first and flicked through: a Google Earth image of our village; a shot of the Play Park taken back before it was rebuilt; the Dairy car park; the Village Bike racks; the front of Rain & Shine Academy. That one was stuck to the next photo, so I peeled them apart with my fingernail. And what I saw made me feel physically sick. It was a picture of my family.

Chapter 29
SPY HQ

WITH THE SOUND of blood thumping in my ears I shakily pulled out the notes, one for each photo. *The Batty family* note was a piece of A4, ripped from a pad, scrawled with Biro:

Thora, 12. Sensitive (lost mother at seven). Medium digital addiction, low activity, poor diet

Reggie, 8. Bright, sometimes needy. High digital addiction, medium activity, poor diet

Shannon, 17. Half sister to Thora & Reggie. Emotionally unstable. Ultra digital addiction, low activity, poor diet

In a red pen, in the margin, someone had added some extra notes:

Watch family closely: lives next door to FF nerve centre. Agent 462 has assigned herself to monitor.

I breathed deeply and looked sideways at Izzy. She hadn't noticed. As I calmed down, I started to feel quite annoyed. I wasn't sensitive for a start, so that was rubbish. I didn't "lose" my mother, it was nothing to do with me.

She died. I didn't have any addictions, digital or otherwise, I walked to school and if I *did* have a poor diet, well that certainly wasn't my fault. Apart from that it was perfect.

They'd got Shannon right, mind you – she definitely had emotional issues. Or at least she used to. Now she had bad acting issues. And another mistake: she was 18.

I flicked on through the folders. The next one was entitled Play Park, then Bikes, Internet, Homelife and so on. The last folder to contain notes was Diet. Each folder had grainy colour images of children eating, reading, playing on the zipwire, even sitting in assembly.

I realised that Izzy and Reggie were looking over my shoulder.

"That's *me,"* whispered Izzy. "In my *bedroom."*

"And there's me! Throwing the paper aeroplanes!"

We looked at each other.

"You see it now, don't you? We're mice. Mice in an experiment," I said, "with Agent 462 looking over our shoulder to make sure we don't step out of line."

"And Dad?" asked Reggie. "He's not on the sheet so he can't be involved, can he?"

"He's up to his neck, Reggie," I said. "I've heard him. He knows everything."

"But why? Why would he allow it?"

Nobody could answer that.

Izzy reached over and flicked through the remaining empty folders. The next one was entitled *Mid-series Assembly Special (Live transmission @ 10.30): Prime Minister.* And underneath: Friday's date.

I wasn't any wiser: why would that horrible man be interested in us? Didn't he have a country to run?

Izzy flicked on; the series of folders continued up to *Week 16: Show Final*. "Week 16! They've hardly started!"

"I don't understand any of it," Reggie said. "What am I addicted to? What are they talking about?"

"Tech," I said. "Tech and modern living. Don't you see? They're making changes, turning it all off, switching us to manual. They want to send us back to the stone age, and everyone's watching them do it."

"But what about our fun?" Reggie asked, stabbing his finger at the Fun Factor logo through the glass. "When are they going to give us some of that?"

Before anyone could try and answer, Charlie shouted from somewhere outside the room. I'd almost forgotten about him. "Hey, that's *my* kitchen! This is amazing! You have *got* to see this."

Reggie ran through to find him.

"Put the folder back like you found it," said Izzy. I turned it over. On the back, someone had written *password1234* in faint pencil, perhaps to remind them of the worst password in the world. I slid the folder back into position.

Izzy and I walked through to the Panopticon and the sight that greeted us took our breath away. Three walls of this large, windowless room were lined with screens, each one the size of a medium TV.

A comfy black chair with a touchscreen mounted in front was positioned on a rotating circular platform in the centre of the room. Reggie and Charlie were squashed in together, with Reggie tapping away at icons on the screen like a budgie in a mirror.

On one wall all the screens were blank except one: on that we could see Mr Moreton, our fearsomely unfriendly caretaker, pushing a mop listlessly up and down a school corridor. All of the other screens displayed a blinking message: 'No motion detected'.

A dozen of the screens on a second wall were active; we could see two children talking on the bench in the Play Park under the floodlights, two waiting outside the shop, and various grown-ups walking home, hunched against the cold.

On the final wall, all of the screens were labelled in the corner: Family 1 in the top left, through to Family 26 bottom right. And on each screen we could peer into a room in that house. Only a couple of the screens were blank: 'Privacy mode enabled'.

This wasn't like CCTV; each picture was crystal clear, in full colour. Most active screens were showing bedrooms, with one or more children lying on their beds reading; one was building a train track, another was fighting with his brother. You could see him shouting, though you couldn't hear him.

"That's Callum," said Charlie, pointing. "Go on Callum, throw him off the bed!"

"Hang on," said Reggie, tapping away at the icons. "I see how this thing works now. It's the same as *TV Simulator 4,* but without the cheat mode. So if we press *this* one... let's hear what he's saying." The sound of Callum's voice rang out, as if he was fighting in the very same room. "I'm gonna get you, Jenson!"

Jenson, squashed underneath Callum, shouted something back that we couldn't hear.

"Yeah, well you deserved it, you told Mrs Scott about my sweets!" A voice called the boys for a drink of milk.

They untangled themselves and left the room, and the camera turned itself off: 'No motion detected'.

"Can they hear us?" whispered Izzy.

"Nah. It'll all be one way, unless you turn this on," said Reggie, tapping a finger microphone.

Charlie chuckled. "Looks like Callum's in trouble with Mrs Scott again."

"Hey look, there's our kitchen!" I pointed up to Family 9, where Dad was busy stirring something revolting on the hob. Melissa was working on her laptop, while Shannon sat opposite, gazing into space and smiling. Then, as we were watching, Shannon looked directly up at the camera... and winked. My blood ran cold.

"What... ? She's seen us!" Izzy cried.

"We should get out of here soon," I said. "This is so wrong."

"No, she can't possibly see us," said Reggie.

"But I still think we should leave," I said, glancing at a red digital clock above the door, which flashed 18:15. "The next show starts in an hour, and I reckon they'll be up here for that."

"They? Who's they?" said Charlie.

"Melissa, definitely," I said.

"Maybe Wharton?" said Izzy.

"Maybe. Definitely Shannon," said Reggie.

"Why would she be here?" I asked. "She's in the notes! She's part of their experiment!"

"What experiment?" asked Charlie.

"I'll explain later," said Reggie to Charlie, who nodded. Patience is one of Charlie's many fine qualities.

"Shannon's definitely in on it," said Reggie. "There are

notes all over the Studio for her. *Sit here Shannon, stand here Shannon, don't look here Shannon*, that kind of thing."

Shannon? A TV presenter? I thought of her silky hair and new beaming smile. It was possible.

Reggie prised himself out of the chair.

"So are we going to blow the place up?" said Charlie.

"What are you talking about?" said Izzy.

"That's what James Bond always does when he leaves the villain's secret underground hideaway. Blows it sky high – kaboom!"

"Yeah well I'd rather you didn't do that, Charlie," I said. "For starters, this secret hideaway isn't very secret, and secondly, it's attached to our house."

"We'll have to be smarter than that," said Reggie. "They'll be on to us as soon as they know we've been up here. We need to attack when they're not concentrating."

"What, like a distraction?" said Izzy.

"A deadly virus?" pondered Charlie. "A poisonous raincloud? A visit from Mr Big? An insect invasion?"

We let Charlie's thoughts hang in the air. Nobody wanted to tell him his suggestions were rubbish.

"Whatever we're planning to do while they're not looking, it has to be done this week," I said, "before the live show. Who knows what'll happen after that. Let's all be quiet for a minute, have a proper think. Then each of us can say our idea, and we'll vote on the one we think is the best."

Everyone nodded.

"OK... go," I said.

I watched the digital clock. Have you ever noticed that the dots in the middle flash with the seconds? And if you count them, you can work out exactly when a minute is...

up.

"Let's hear everyone's ideas then."

"Ideas for what?" asked Charlie.

I sighed. "Ideas for ending this madness," I said. "For getting our normal lives back. Right, Izzy, you first."

"What, me? Why me first? Why not you?"

"Because I'm the oldest, and I'm in charge. OK, Reggie, you go."

"Well... " said Reggie. "It's not going to be easy."

"I'll go first," interrupted Charlie. "I've got an amazing plan."

"Hmm," I said. "Let's hear it then."

"So we know that all the grown-ups are spies, right? And they're probably from North Korea or somewhere. But they're bound to need spy messages from HQ, they always do. So we get one in a room and tie them up, and then..."

"Yeah OK Charlie, not sure that's going to happen," I said.

"But I haven't told you the best bit! Because when they confess we nick their clothes and pretend to be them so we can find out what their instructions are. Simple. And then we – "

"Blow the place sky high?" I guessed.

"Yes!" Charlie beamed. "You know my plan!"

"Got it," I said. Sometimes it's easier to go along with Charlie. "Just *supposing* that doesn't work out, does anyone have any other ideas?"

Izzy scuffed the ground with her foot. Charlie picked his nose. Reggie looked up at the ceiling, as if there might be a plan floating there if he stared hard enough.

"Well," I said. "It looks like we risked our lives for

nothing. They're going to do their 'mid-series special' with the Prime Minister, whatever that is, and we've got months and months more of this misery, and then who knows what comes next. And all we can do is know that they're watching us, and wish we could think of a good way to stop them." Charlie opened his mouth. "Apart from Charlie's plan, of course, and that won't work. Well this is rubbish, that's what it is."

The feeling of disappointment was crushing. I thought we were a team, a gang who could make things happen. Turns out we were four losers without a clue.

"We'll come up with something," said Reggie. "We've got until Friday I guess. It's only Tuesday."

"But we haven't even got the beginnings of a plan!"

"It'll be fine," said Izzy. "We just need to do our homework."

"Homework?!" I nearly exploded. "What use is the bus stop method of division when grown-ups are making your life a misery?"

"Shh, Thora, relax," said Izzy. "Come on, I need to get home."

And that, it seemed, was the end of the meeting.

We glumly retraced our steps out of the Panopticon and down the stairs, being careful to put everything back exactly as we'd found it. I switched off the lights, plunging the upstairs into darkness. Charlie peeled the jelly hand off the sensor and I was careful to take it from him in case he was tempted to give it a nibble. Izzy gave the glass panel a rub with her sleeve.

And with a quick vow of secrecy and a promise to meet again the following day we traipsed home.

Chapter 30
MY PLAN

MEETING AGAIN AFTER school wasn't that easy. Wherever you stood in the village you'd look up and see a camera. In the end we grabbed bikes and headed down to the dairy car park. After docking our bikes ("they might have microphones in them," warned Reggie) we found a quiet corner behind the old building. But I don't know why we bothered. Nobody had anything new to say except Charlie, and nobody was in the mood to hear his high explosive plans.

We crouched in silence and despair, staring out at the rapidly filling car park.

"That's odd," I said. "Look. Why are they going that way?"

A thin stream of people was splitting off from the main crowd and disappearing around the back of the dairy, many of them looking around furtively as they did so.

"Who knows. Shortcut?" said Reggie.

I shook my head.

"I'm off home," said Reggie.

"I think I'll hang here a bit," I said.

Reggie shrugged. "Come on, let's go. There are hardly any bikes left." And they left me. And that was just fine, even when all the bikes were gone half an hour later, forcing me to join the grown-ups for the long trudge home.

Reggie was still grumpy when I got home but that was OK, too. I had too much to think about, lying under my scratchy blanket, staring towards the sensor in the dark. I waved to set it off, the red light pinging on. And I imagined unseen, unknown figures watching me from the Panopticon next door, disappointed when nothing happened.

In Wednesday's assembly, to the surprise of everyone except our little gang, Frosty announced that lunch would be a bit later on Friday because we would be having a special mid-morning assembly to announce the winner of the Tidy Classroom Cup.

It's worth explaining that every week Mr Moreton, the grumpy caretaker that everyone called "The Jailer" because of his jangling bunch of keys, would shuffle to the front and hand over a Tidy Classroom certificate to that week's winner. Class 8S often won because Mrs Scott was always nagging us about it.

You'd think Mr Moreton would be happy about this weekly ritual since we were making his life easier. But every week he scowled at the winner as if he was being asked to hand over his salary, not a piece of card with a "Tidy Terrapin" cartoon on it. I think he just hated being told to come out of his stinky cupboard where he sat with his mops and his brooms, drinking tea and reading the paper.

But Frosty wasn't talking about a certificate here: this was the first any of us had heard about a Tidy Classroom

Cup. But that was fine: in fact it was better than fine. It might be the answer I was looking for, although for now I turned Izzy and Reggie's questions away; I was still turning ideas over in my head. And that's where they were going to stay, hidden a little while longer.

"Thora! Thora!" It was Reggie, whispering from his bed that night. "Talk to me!"

"Sorry, Reggie, I'm thinking. But I've nearly finished, maybe."

"Do you have a plan?"

"Maybe. I don't know. Ask me in the morning."

And with that I turned over and fell straight to sleep.

My fingers were aching, my bum was numb, and I was cold. It turns out that houses get quite chilly at night. And you'll particularly feel it if you sit on the floor in your nightie for two hours writing on index cards. But there they were: four piles, each with a name on top, held together with a rubber band.

"Thora!"

I almost jumped out of my skin at the sound of Reggie's voice.

"Have you –"

I turned to him from my spot in the corner, tucked behind the wardrobe and out of sight of the camera, and held my finger to my lips. I bundled the piles of cards up in my school uniform and went to the bathroom to get dressed.

At break time I pulled the gang into a huddle behind

197

the bins.

"Where have you been, Thora?" asked Charlie. "Have you got a plan?"

The others looked at me nervously. I could feel that familiar burning heat of a spotlight, the crushing weight of their expectation, the sensation of being wound up too tightly... But somehow, this time, it felt a little bit different. It took me a moment to recognise the feeling, because it was so similar: it was excitement.

"Yes. But now it's your turn," I said with a confidence I didn't completely feel. I handed each of them a stack of cards with their names written neatly on the top. "This is the POA. Hide it now. Read it in your bathroom later."

"What's a POA?" asked Izzy. "And why do we have to read it in the bathroom?"

"Plan Of Action," I said. Two could play at this spy talk. "And the bathroom is the only place in your house without cameras. It's how we're going to blow this thing apart."

"Cool," said Charlie. "But why do we want to blow up a bathroom?"

"Not literally," I said. Izzy looked relieved. "No, it's better than that. Tomorrow, everything changes. But you need to know your part, then rip the plan into pieces and flush it down the toilet."

Charlie was peering at his cards. "I've only got one thing to do," he said.

"Yes, but nobody else can do it," I said.

"You can rely on me, Thora. I'm going to go home, learn it and then use the card to wipe my bottom. Nobody will be able to read it then."

Izzy made a noise like she was being sick.

"Remember, everyone, this will only work if you do *exactly* what it says on the cards. Do you trust me?" I held out my hand.

"I trust you, Thora," Reggie said solemnly, placing his hand on mine.

"Me too," said Izzy.

"Me three," said Charlie, joining the stack of hands. "You're the man with the plan."

The school bell rang for the end of break. I made sure that we had all tucked our cards out of sight, and we headed for the door.

On the way back I sneaked into the toilets to rehearse. I'd written out my part like I was one of the others, to keep everything separate in my head. That way, when I was following instructions, I could forget that they were written by me.

On my first card was instruction number 1:

Tidy the classroom, but make sure Mrs Scott sees you doing it.

So at afternoon break I hung behind, and set to work. I tidied up the coloured pencils, and sharpened the blunt ones. I threw away the drawing scraps and stacked the topic books. I lined up the chairs and tables in neat rows, and pinned back the flapping poster of Iron Age Britain, the one that Mrs Scott had put up after she took down the 'E-safety' pictures. Then, as I was running out of things to do, I saw Mrs Scott returning with her cup of tea.

As she entered I started walking towards the door to the playground.

"Well, well!" she said. "Thora – was this your hard work?"

I stopped, and turned. "Yes, Mrs Scott. I thought it was a bit messy, and y'know, with the special Tidy Classroom Cup tomorrow..."

"How commendable!" she exclaimed. "A tidy classroom means a tidy – "

"Mind," I said, completing her catchphrase.

"That's right. Now get yourself a bit of fresh air, you've earned it."

"Thanks Mrs Scott!" I said, running outside.

I stopped dead in my tracks; my heart was pounding and I felt dizzy, but in a good way. This was it, we'd started. There was no going back now.

Chapter 31
AND THE WINNER IS...

FRIDAY: THE BIG day. I'd been up until late the previous night, reading my cards, going over the *ifs* and *buts* in my mind. Reggie had gone straight to sleep which worried me: he had a lot to get right.

But I hadn't got time to worry about that now. I turned off my alarm clock at the first chime, shook Reggie awake and we slid quietly out of the house. Without a word, Reggie disappeared up the path into Enid's house holding his roll of packing tape and a large jelly hand.

The village was deserted; not even the dog walkers were up yet. I thought about taking a bike but decided it was too risky. So I set out on the longest run of my life, right out of the village and down to the dairy. Panting heavily, I arrived at the handprint sensor that controlled the fierce metal teeth in the road. From now on, I'd have to make things up as I went along.

I had a small rucksack with me, filled with things I thought might help. Firstly, to check I knew what I was doing, I put my hand on the sensor.

"Entry denied," said a flat American voice. As expected. Then I pulled out Melissa's other jelly hand and slapped it on the sensor.

201

"Proceed." With a metallic grating noise the teeth descended into the road, and then rose again a moment later.

Right. Time to cut this village off properly. I pulled out some kitchen scissors. If I could find the right wire, I could be on my way in seconds. But all the inner workings of the sensor were completely encased in metal, and the post had been concreted into the ground – no chance of simply pushing it over. As I feared.

My next idea was a genius touch, I thought. A few years back – before Shannon decided she was too cool for our family – she played an April Fool's trick on Dad, covering the bowl of the toilet with cling film. A fuzzy-eyed Dad had gone for an early morning wee and then shouted in horror as the wee bounced off in all directions, spraying the bathroom.

With that in mind (sort of), I tore off a piece of film and carefully smoothed it over the surface of the fingerprint scanner, squishing out the air bubbles until it was nearly invisible. Holding my breath, I held Melissa's hand to the scanner.

"Proceed." My heart sank at the same time as the metal teeth.

I was nearly out of ideas, and the last one wasn't ideal. I'm not a natural vandal. Reggie would have found 14 ways to destroy the post by now, but I'd rather leave things as I find them. But when the government is threatening to ruin your life for ever, I think a little rebellion is allowed. Pulling out a small bottle of Shannon's black nail varnish (she wasn't using *that* any more), I painted patches all over the dark touchscreen. As I hoped it was hard to spot, not that it really mattered.

The sun had crept above the fells and it was getting warm now – people would be walking down from the village to pick up their cars for work soon. I didn't have time to wait until the polish dried. For the first but definitely not the last time, I crossed my fingers.

By the time I got back to the house and crept back up the stairs, sweaty and exhausted, Reggie was already in Dad's bedroom, complaining about his poorly tummy. By the time I was ready for school, he was back in bed.

"Get some rest," Melissa said gently, tucking him in. "I'm out this morning, but Shannon's on study leave so I've told her to keep an eye on you until your Dad's back at lunchtime."

Reggie's eyes were shut – screwed tight shut – but from where I was standing, hidden from Melissa's view, I could see a little thumb sticking up from under the blankets.

I tried to play games in the playground before school, but I found it hard to concentrate and Izzy wasn't there to talk to – or Charlie, for that matter. I finally felt like a secret agent, but one who had been sent on a deadly mission into enemy territory while everyone else was back at base, comfy, warm and eating toast.

At quarter to ten we filed into the main hall for the special assembly. Everyone around me chattered excitedly: a rumour was going around that 8S was about to scoop the Tidy Classroom Cup. On stage, Frosty was strutting around in a peacock green suit with an orange bow tie, bouncing on his toes and crouching to grin wildly at the unfortunate little reception children who sat right in front of him.

Staff filed in with their classes and joined the other grown-ups in the chairs that ran along the walls. Kristi stood alongside the stage in place of Mr Wharton, just as I expected. She was smiling nervously at nothing in particular.

Frosty saw her and frowned. "Where's Geoff?" he mouthed.

Kristi mimed driving, crossed her arms and frowned, made a face like a tiger with bared white teeth, and then shook her head. It was like the worst game of charades you've ever seen.

Frosty looked at her like she was an idiot, which was fair enough. Then she pointed to her ear – the one we couldn't see – and gave a thumbs up, which didn't seem to reassure him at all.

Mr Frost held up his arms and waited for quiet.

"Good Morning, Shiners!"

"Good morning, Mr Frost, Good morning everyone," we droned.

"And a big welcome to you all on this momentous day," said Frosty. "Sadly, Mr Wharton can't join us this morning. He's been held up; Kristi here tells me that he crashed into a lion on the way to work." The reception children tittered. "Still, I'm sure he'll come *roaring* in as soon as he can, eh children?" Frosty smiled at us and then looked witheringly at Kristi, who was hopping from one foot to the other, a manic grin plastered across her face.

"This is a very special assembly. As you know, very

soon we'll be announcing the winners of the first ever Tidy Classroom Cup!"

A few children whooped and cheered.

Frosty was into his stride now and appeared even more animated than normal. He waved his arms and stalked around the stage, eyes darting everywhere.

"And it gets better. I'm very excited to tell you that at half past ten a *very* special visitor will be congratulating the winning class, live via our big screen." I breathed out with relief; it was just as I'd guessed. He bent his knees and raised his palms to the ceiling, and we all made a "Whoooo!" noise like he wanted us to. "A very special visitor, very special indeed. We are so lucky."

Children looked at each other in puzzlement.

There was a reading and we sang a couple of hymns; as usual, Frosty nearly drowned us out with his tuneless voice booming out over our own. He took to the stage again.

"OK children, this is it. The big one. The Tidy Classroom Cup. Are we ready?"

"Yes!" everyone shouted. Frosty looked over our heads at the adults.

"I said, are you ready?" Frosty threw up his hands, a crazy grin on his face.

"YES!" everyone shouted, so loud that a couple of reception children started to cry. It was as if he was appearing in an episode of his own game show. Maybe he was.

Frosty looked at Kristi, and then up at the clock: 10.20. "Looks like we're all set," said Frosty, looking slightly nervous for the first time. "Now then, there's only one person who can judge this new award, so let's get him up on stage. Please put your hands together and give a big Rain & Shine clapporama to our one and only caretaking hero, Mr Moreton!"

We all clapped dutifully as The Jailer lumbered on stage and stood glowering at us. For once he didn't have his keys, perhaps to avoid deafening us with the jingle jangle.

"Well, I don't need to tell you it's been a very close run thing, hasn't it Mr Moreton?"

The Jailer wrinkled his nose.

"We've seen some sterling efforts around school, but at the end of the day there was one clear winner. One class that really went the extra mile, pulled out the stops, went for broke and put their heart and soul into it."

Frosty never said one word when he could vomit a whole dictionary. He was prolonging the agony and he knew it. But what he didn't know was that we were about to discover if we'd be released from this crazy experiment, or condemned to a miserable fun-free life for ever.

Frosty pulled an envelope out of his shiny green suit pocket. "I must do this properly," he said, opening it. "And so I'm thrilled to announce that the first winners of the Tidy Classroom cup are... " Frosty paused, grinning. "Class FOUR – "

My heart hit the floor. It was over. Year 4? The plan was dead, life would never be normal again. All the Year 4 kids were screaming, not sure which of their classes had won.

"Only kidding with you," he said. "Though 4D did

do a fantastic job. Class 4J not so much. The real winners were TWO – "

He paused. I could hardly breathe. "No, my mistake, sorry Year 2. It's Class 8S!"

There were gasps, cheers and applause. Mrs Scott beamed with pride at the end of our row.

"Worthy winners, I'm sure we all agree, and I understand they clinched the award with a last-minute show of initiative, is that right, Mrs Scott?"

Mrs Scott nodded, smiling.

"Perhaps you'd like to send up your most tidy-minded class member to receive the cup, and greet our special visitor."

I looked at Mrs Scott, smiling but feeling like I was going to be sick. Her eyes darted up and down the row of thrusting hands. She looked directly at me and nodded. I got unsteadily to my feet. Mrs Scott patted me on the back as I passed, and Frosty helped me up onto the stage.

"Thora Batty, you and your class are the pride of Rain & Shine Academy," Frosty said, grasping my hand and pumping it up and down like he was trying to draw water from a deep well. "But before we present you with the cup and you get to meet our special visitor, we have something for everyone to enjoy."

Frosty looked over at the Jailor and smiled – a smile which wasn't returned.

"For the last week, Mr Moreton has been kindly wearing a little camera, hidden in his sweatshirt – you could call it a Caretaker Cam, couldn't you Mr Morton?"

Mr Moreton squinted and looked at Frosty as if he'd rather be cleaning the boys' toilets.

"And so with the aid of our Caretaker Cam and help from the Academy's IT whizzes, we've made a special film all about our tidy school!"

A film all about the insides of the Jailor's stinky cupboard, more like. I'm surprised they found film of anything else on there.

Frosty gestured to the side, so I stood next to the Jailor. I could smell him, a strange combination of stinky man and bleach.

"So can we have the big screen switched on please, and let's see what happened!" Frosty put down the microphone on a small table and stood legs apart, facing the school, confident that he knew exactly what would be appearing on the screen behind him. But he was wrong.

Chapter 32
LOCKED IN

"THAT'S MY MUM!"

Who knows who shouted first. A boy in Year 3, I think, and everyone around him laughed like drains. Because the first picture we saw definitely wasn't of Rain & Shine's overflowing bins, the Jailor's stinky den or the boys' toilets. It was a woman in a kitchen, clearing away the breakfast things. We couldn't hear her, but we could see her face stretched into crazy expressions. She put down the cereal packet and picked up a bottle of juice, using it as a microphone.

Facing away from the screen, Frosty didn't realise what was going on and chuckled along with us. But staff along the edges were pointing and trying to stifle their laughs.

The mum picked up an air guitar and played a solo, prompting more laughter. Frosty frowned, and turned just as the picture changed. It was the outside of Rain & Shine: the empty car park. Flick: now the village green. Flick: the inside of the Reflection Room. Seeing nothing wrong, Frosty turned back and gestured at us to calm down.

Behind him, flick: another mum, this time hoovering the stairs. "Mummy!" shouted one of the reception kids, her arms stretched out to the screen. Flick: a dad sat at the kitchen table, playing patience. Flick: a mum gardening. Flick: two older kids at the play park. Flick: a girl in her bedroom, playing with her dolls. "That's Charlotte!" said a Year 5. "She's supposed to be off sick!" Oh dear. Looked like Charlotte was in trouble.

By now the whole school was shrieking and pointing. Nobody was taking any notice of our headteacher, spinning his arms like a windmill at the noise we were making. Snapshots of grown-ups and views inside and outside village houses were flashing past now. Kristi, who had been shrieking and pointing from the side of the hall, ran on stage and yanked Frosty around to face the screen. He jerked as if he'd had an electric shock, and looked to the back of the hall. "Cut, cut, cut!" he screamed, drawing his hand across his throat. It would have been a scary gesture if he hadn't accidentally twizzled his bow tie right around.

I looked to the back of the room. Miss Priti, who was in charge of "pressing the buttons", as Frosty called it, wasn't having a good day. With a helpless, panicked expression she was holding her precious remote control at arm's length, stabbing it again and again with her thumb. She didn't know that it would have to beam right across the village and into the Panopticon to have any effect.

"Make it stop!" Frosty thundered above the chaos.

"I can't!" she screamed back. "I've lost control!"

You could say that again.

Kristi looked as if she'd walked into a spelling test and found out she'd been learning the wrong words. And since she was managing to achieve precisely nothing in the hall, she evidently decided to make a run for it through the double doors. The locked double doors, as it turned out.

"Mr Moreton, open those doors immediately!" Frosty boomed.

The Jailor smiled for the first time. "Don't you remember, Mr Frost?" he said, raising his voice to be heard above the screaming children. "You told me not to bring my keys." He shrugged before looking around as if he were watching a mildly entertaining quiz show.

Kristi spotted the doors on the opposite side. She sprinted along the row of Year 2s who shouted and complained as she trampled on their toes and grabbed onto the tops of their heads for support. Slam! She threw herself against the door before withdrawing and rubbing her shoulder.

What we saw through the round glass window was a surprise to everyone, including me: it was Sheila, the lollipop lady. She was grinning broadly, her head waggling and her curly hair bouncing. With one hand she gave me a big thumbs up, and in the other, held up for all to see, were the Jailor's keys.

Mr Moreton didn't like that one bit. Now he roared, but his was just one more roar in the zoo: everyone had something to shout about, it seemed.

Meanwhile on screen the sequence of village pictures had ended. In its place we could now see Shannon. She was sat on one of the studio sofas, a pile of papers on her lap. She was deep in concentration, reading her notes. She clearly didn't have a clue that we could see her.

Frosty noticed her. "What the heck is she doing up there?" he yelled, to nobody in particular.

"Who is it?" said a little girl in reception closest to me.

"That's my sister," I said. "She thinks she's going to be

211

on telly. And in a way, she is."

The little girl nodded as if that made perfect sense, and went back to inspecting the bogey she'd dragged out of her nose.

While the craziness unfolded I steeled myself: it was time to move onto Index Card Three of The Plan. Unnoticed by anyone, it seemed, I walked across and picked up the microphone.

I tapped it cautiously. A thud could be heard above the uproar.

"Excuse me," I said. Nobody took any notice.

"Excuse Me."

Nothing.

I put my mouth right up against the microphone. "CAN EVERYONE PAY ATTENTION FOR A MOMENT PLEASE?" The speakers shrieked and whined.

That worked: the room was shocked into silence. On screen, Shannon held up a compact mirror, still blissfully unaware, and touched up her make-up.

This was me, Thora Batty, speaking to a room of more than 200 people. Rows and rows of eyes, all fixed on me, waiting to see what I would say next. And though I didn't know what I'd say next, my mouth did. So I opened it, and the words tumbled out.

"I'm sorry you're not going to see Mr Moreton's Bin Film," I said. I paused, just like Frosty does, and everyone waited in complete silence. You could have heard steam escaping from a pie at the factory down the valley. "I've heard that it was rubbish, anyway." It turns out anyone can make bad jokes like Frosty. And I had one fan, at least: for a second, a small smile crossed Mr Moreton's face.

I shuffled my index cards nervously. I could barely read my own writing. "Instead you're going to see something different. A new TV show."

There were whoops at the mention of the word TV. Frosty and Kristi had frozen, like children playing Musical Statues. They looked as if they were waiting for instructions, but from whom it wasn't clear.

The sound of my own voice was strangely reassuring, as if hearing The Plan put into words made it feel like it was going to succeed.

"So this TV show has a glamorous presenter you should meet, called Shannon. Let's say hello." I paused to give Reggie time to feed my voice through to the studio. "Hello Shannon!"

On screen, Shannon's arm jolted as if someone had knocked her, and lipstick streaked across her cheek. The camera zoomed in on her face.

"What?" she shrieked. "What's going on? We're not due on air for ten minutes! You're early! Turn the camera off!"

At the sight of my sister my butterfly nerves disappeared entirely. I didn't need an index card for this: I knew exactly how to speak to her. "Calm down Shannon, you're not on live TV yet, unless you count Rain & Shine Academy," I said. "Say hello, Rain & Shine Academy!"

"Hello Shannon!" everyone hollered.

"Thora? Is that you?" said Shannon, peering into the camera as if she could see me. "Speak to me! Thora! What are you doing! Thora!"

"Thanks Reggie, that's enough of Shannon for now," I said. "Selfie time."

The picture cut to Reggie, waving to a camera from his revolving chair in the Panopticon. I could see his pile of index cards stacked up on the desk: good boy. "Hello everyone!" he yelled.

The hall went crazy: whoever else they expected to see on screen, it wasn't an eight-year-old from Year 3 in an *Ogre Smackdown* hoodie.

Meanwhile Frosty had abandoned his zombie impression. "Reggie Batty!" he roared. It seemed he didn't like other people running his assembly – particularly an impertinent girl called Thora and her trusting brother Reggie. "You're both in on this fiasco!"

With three giant bounds he crossed the stage and lunged for the microphone. I grabbed onto it tightly, holding it to my chest. The green-suited loudmouth grappled me to the ground and tried to pull it from my arms, bellowing like a wounded buffalo right in my ear.

"Cut now, Reggie! Link us up! Go! Go! Go!"

Just as Frosty got his hands on the microphone a chorus of gasps went up from the audience.

"Oh wow!" said someone.

"Isn't that...?" shouted a teacher.

"What's he *doing*?" said Mr Moreton.

"Are those actually his pants?" said Mrs Priti.

"Let her go, Frosty," said Reggie over the speakers in a slightly squeaky voice. That's bravery for you: everyone knew he hated being called Frosty. "Let my sister go or I'll show the whole country what you can see."

As soon as Frosty saw the screen his arms went floppy, like a tiger hit by a vet's anaesthetic dart. I scrambled to my feet, microphone still in hand.

"Snakes alive," Frosty said quietly, still lying on the stage. The shout appearing to have left him entirely. "Yes," he whispered, so I could barely hear him. "Yes, I believe those *are* his actual pants.'

Chapter 33
SHOW TIME

THE ROOM WE could all see on screen wasn't much to look at. The walls were panelled with dark wood. The tall, deep window was draped with depressing curtains and didn't let in much light, while the tired carpet wouldn't have looked out of place in a run-down library. The room was dominated by a large, leather-topped desk. A laptop, lamp and piles of papers took up most of the space. The rest of it was taken up by a fat man in Superman underpants cutting his toenails while playing Juicy Bubbles on his mobile phone.

The younger children probably didn't even know what the Prime Minister looked like. But whether you knew this was the most important man in the country or not, there was no denying that this made unmissable telly.

The revolting man grimaced as he tackled a particularly horny old toenail, and then sighed with satisfaction as it pinged off across the room. He hurriedly tapped on the phone next to him to stop his bubbles popping.

From the waist up, he was the picture of respectability, the kind of chap you see every day on the news: his bouffant blonde hair was swept to one side, his red face was shiny but clean-looking. A crisp white shirt was doing a marvellous job, every button working as a team to contain his bulging belly. An expensive-looking tie started in the right place at his neck, but lost its way and trailed off under his armpit.

This walrus of a man was sitting on the desk with his knees bent up either side of his belly, his heels resting against the laptop – presumably the only way he could reach his hairy feet with the nail scissors.

If you've ever sat that way for long – even if you don't have a belly like a water balloon – you'll know that your pants can end up where they shouldn't, riding up your bottom. So he did as anyone would do, and hoiked his greying Superman pants out with his finger.

For the second time, the hall was quiet: hundreds of jaws hung open in amazement. There was the occasional *ping!* as a bubble popped on the Prime Minister's phone, and a *snick!* sound as another toenail clipping rocketed off out of view. "Ah blitheration!" we heard him mutter as he lost his last bubble life and started another game.

"Agent 369 calling Top Dog, over." Back in the hall, someone was talking. "Agent 369 calling Top Dog, do you read me?" Louder now. I looked to the back of the room: Kristi had crept to the back, and was now crouching down holding a walkie-talkie.

"CALLING TOP DOG! YOU NEED TO GET THE STUDIO SHUT DOWN RIGHT NOW, THE PRIME MINISTER IS ON THE TELLY IN HIS PANTS!" she screamed.

The radio crackled. "This is Top Dog. Calm down Kristi. We're not live until 10.30. I don't know what you're gibbering on about, but I'm on my way round right now, we'll be there in a jiffy." It was the unmistakable toffee tones of Mr Wharton.

"Sounds like trouble, Reggie," I said quietly into the microphone. "Wharton's coming."

While Rain & Shine Academy watched the nation's leader get a high score and clear out his toe jam, Reggie tapped at his computer. "Hang on, let's have a look. No... he's not there... not there either... Ah! Got him."

"Where is he, Reggie? Is he on foot?"

"I've picked him up on the main road. He's got hold of a buggy somehow," Reggie said. That was worrying. "He's turned right... looks like he's heading towards Enid's."

"If he gets to the Studio and pulls the plug we're stuffed," I said.

"Stick to the plan, Thora," said Reggie with confidence. "You've done your homework. Wharton won't get past Charlie. You get on with the show."

The PM had finished his nails now, and had lifted his shirt and vest up. With one hand he was stretching his belly; with the index finger of the other he was trying to reach in and hook out the fluff from his tummy button. The effort was immense, and you could hear him grunting.

"The show! Get on with the show!" some of the kids were now chanting.

"Get on with it!" shouted Mr Brown, head of PE. The teachers and children all seemed to be enjoying the performance immensely, even though I'd guess that none of them knew what was going on. None of them were lifting a finger to help Kristi, who was now slumped in a chair, defeated.

I turned to the next index card. There was one word, in big capital letters: IMPROVISE.

Yes. Slight problem. I had a sudden flashback to the previous morning, sitting in my nightie on the cold floor, trying to think what I'd do once the Prime Minister was on screen. And I'd got so excited by what would happen next that I, err, forgot to work it out. I'd have to make it up.

"Ah yes, ah, the show!" I said into the microphone. "So I was saying, there's a new TV show in town, and I, err, I want to tell you all about it!" I waited nervously, the PM still on screen. "So any time soon we'll go back to the Studio... now, Reggie, now!" I whispered.

"Sorry!" called Reggie over the speakers, and flipped the picture back to Shannon, who was lying on her back on the studio sofa. Slowly, Reggie brought the FF logo on the back wall into focus.

"Boys and girls, welcome to... The Fun Factor!"

With a crash of cymbals and a blast of trumpets, an ear-splitting tune filled the air. At the sound of the cymbals Shannon raised her head, realised that nothing had changed and lay back down. Clarinets trilled to the beat of a big bass drum before a crescendo of trombones wrapped up with a musical "ta-da!'. The music faded into the sound of an unseen studio audience laughing uproariously. On and on and on they laughed, sounding more ominous, more mocking with every second. Reception children started to look tearful and cover their ears. Just in time, Reggie faded the music out.

"Eh?" said one child.

"What was that?"

"What's Fun Factor?"

"Who was laughing? Were they laughing at us?"

Children around the hall were turning to each other, puzzled. I gave them a minute to chat.

"You've never heard of it, right?" I said. I was getting the hang of this now. Two hundred children shook their head at me. "There are two good reasons for that. The first reason is that the grown-ups took away all you tellies, your tablets, your phones and your consoles."

"Boo!" everyone shouted, back on form, like they were at the pantomime.

I waited for a bit, until I could be heard. "And the second reason is that you're *not meant* to watch this show. Even though the whole country is watching it, every night, you're not allowed to see it. Because then you'd find out that The Fun Factor is all about... you."

Well, you've never heard such a noise. Everyone went *wild*. Some of the teachers stood up, looking alarmed. I raised my hands for quiet again, just like Frosty would have done if he had been in charge instead of having his head stroked by Mrs Maynard, the school secretary.

"Thora. Thora," interrupted Reggie.

"What is it, Reggie? I'm about to explain."

"The PM's getting a bit argy-bargy. I think one of us needs a word. Hang on, I'll flip you over."

"Right, what's going on here? I thought you were hooking me up to that Stain and Whine school so I could talk to some revolting children. Is this thing on? Somebody speak to me!"

The Prime Minister was now sat behind his desk. He'd swept the toenail clippings onto the carpet, hidden his phone and was now peering towards the camera, his bushy eyebrows jumping up and down like excited gerbils.

"Hold fire, Prime Minister," we heard Reggie say. "We're a bit busy. We'll be with you in a minute."

"Who the devil is that?" thundered the Prime Minister. "You sound like you're about 11! Nobody tells me to wait. No wonder it's going pear-shaped. Get me a professional!"

"I'm eight, actually," said Reggie. "My name's Reggie, and I *am* a professional."

"I assume that's some kind of joke, but rest assured it's the last one you'll ever make. You'll be lucky if you're allowed to make the tea by the end of the day. Now what the jimminy is going on in that godforsaken spot? I've got important business to get on with!"

"Patience please." I was in awe: my little brother, telling the Prime Minister to chill out. "Thora is introducing the children to The Fun Factor. They have a bit of catching up to do."

"Who the blazes is Thora, dare I ask?" thundered the PM, slamming his meaty fist on the desk. "Let me guess, is it producer Reggie's great grandmother, taking a break from the bingo? No, don't answer that! And what do you mean, you're telling them about Fun Factor? That's the whole point! They're not allowed to know! I might have failed my SATs or whatever you call them these days but even I know that! You're an idiot! A prize idiot!"

"Calm down," said Reggie. "There's no need to shout."

"You don't tell the Prime Minister to calm down! You're fired, you little squirt! Get me the boss of the BBC!" The PM leaped out of his seat but then realised we could see his pants, so he sat down again quickly. But his face was strawberry red and a shower of spit sprayed over his desk as he spoke.

"Prime Minister," I said, my voice wobbling. I felt that Reggie had done his best. Sometimes, big sisters have to *be* big sisters. "If I could interrupt you for a moment. You might want to look at your monitor. I want to show you what we could see five minutes ago."

The PM jutted his face forward, peering at the playback on the camera. "What the... how the... why would you have filmed *that?*"

"It would make a great newsflash, don't you think? The PM getting on with some important bubble business in his pants? Live across the nation's TV screens?"

"But... that's blackmail!" the PM whispered into the camera. His crimson face filled the screen, his eyes darting here there and everywhere as if he was trying to spot us through the lens. "You're blackmailing me! You wouldn't dare, you little pipsqueak!"

"Yes we would," I said. "And you won't take the risk. So if you'll excuse me, I need to explain a few things to Rain & Shine Academy. You sit back, pop a few bubbles, have a listen."

And with that my brother abruptly switched off the raging PM and the screen went blank. "Thanks Reggie, and welcome back!" A warm feeling started in my tummy and spread rapidly, rising to my head where I felt almost dizzy. I was *enjoying* this. I put down my Index Cards and skipped to the middle of the stage.

"Reggie – can you show the parent payment screen?"

Reggie tip-tapped for a moment. "Which class?"

I looked out, and saw a row of my classmates at the

back. "Give me class 8S."

Two rows of passport photos appeared, a bit like a digital version of *Guess Who?* My dad was at the end of the first row. My class all screamed in delight to see their parents on screen.

"Which parent?" asked Reggie.

"Show them Dad," I said. "It's only fair."

Reggie tapped on our Dad's head, and a big bar graph appeared, one bar for each week. I know, more maths, and this time Izzy wasn't there to explain. But this one told a different story. Under most weeks was the figure £1,500.

"So this is why your stuff has disappeared. This is why ice cream isn't on the menu. This is why we're all on bikes, and there are no TV channels. They asked your parents, and they said yes: we'll turn our children into guinea pigs for your experiment. And we'll let you make a TV show out if it, and you can call it The Fun Factor... but only if you pay us £1,500 per week. Plus bonus."

There was a stunned silence.

Reggie tapped and we were back at the *Guess Who?* screen, except now each parent had a "Total Earnings" figure beneath their picture. Numbers ranged from £17,100 (that was Jackson's dad: we hadn't seen Jackson for half the term because he'd been in America), right up to an amazing £99,300 (under Izzy's mum, of course).

"Whoah. Aaah." That was the sound of 200 children breathing out in astonishment. (Well, maybe not the reception children as they're not good with numbers.)

"They're not all the same, because sometimes we didn't always behave like good little guinea pigs." Reggie tapped Dad's column and a list of penalties appeared:

Privacy mode left active: **-£300**
Low physical activity: **-£100**
Disclosure of confidential information: **-£1,000**

(The list went on... it seemed that Reggie and I had been very naughty guinea pigs.)

The room was buzzing now; not chaotic like before, but full of children asking each other questions, swapping pieces of the puzzle.

I cleared my throat, and slowly the children became quieter.

"There's another mystery though. Haven't you wondered why our parents seem to manage just fine without their phones? Without email, without YouTube, without Facebook?" A sea of nonplussed faces stared back at me. "Because that's the other demand our parents made: one rule for you, one rule for them. And to explain *that*, we need to go live to our special reporter, Izzy. Izzy, can you hear me?"

Chapter 34
IZZY'S MOMENT

GO LIVE.

I was so proud to say that, I felt like a proper TV reporter now. Reggie was spot on with his timing this time, flicking the screen to Izzy. She was standing down by the village barrier; someone had put some old carpet over the teeth in the road to make a ramp – Mr Wharton, I guessed. It seemed a very long time since I'd been there with a bottle of nail polish early that morning.

Over Izzy's left shoulder we could see a cow on the verge, chewing lazily at some long grass. Izzy appeared to be holding the camera out in front of her, selfie-style.

"I can hear you, Thora!" she said with a nervous smile.

"Who the bloomin heck is Izzy?" thundered the Prime Minister in the background. "Has the world gone mad? How do I –"

"Reggie! The PM's back!" I said under my breath.

"Sorry...." The PM's voice faded away. "That should do it," muttered Reggie. "Back to you, Izzy."

"Hi everyone! I'm Izzy from 8S, but then you probably know that. So I want to ask you a question." Izzy looked down at her index card. "Do you know where your parents are?"

Children in the hall turned to each other and most of them nodded.

"Because I bet some of them aren't where you think. And I'm going to show you."

By now Izzy was walking across the car park to the old dairy. She turned the camera round so we could see what she could see, and entered a narrow gap between the buildings.

"But before I do *that*," she whispered, "take a look at this."

The right hand wall of the alleyway was made of breeze blocks, the left was corrugated iron, thick with moss. Izzy stopped where a sheet had slipped sideways and poked the camera through the hole. A school-full of children squinted, trying to make sense of the gloomy scene.

It seemed to be some kind of low-ceilinged warehouse; double doors at the far end let in enough light for the camera to focus. On the left we could see two rows of familiar white golf buggies, the distinctive red spots visible in the low light. But on the right was a mirror image: a row of shadows. They were the shape of golf buggies, but without any internal features. Izzy trained the camera on the closest buggy but the camera whirred and zoomed in vain, unable to make anything of this big chunk of nothingness. A hole in the landscape – the kind of thing you'd see from your bedroom window in the depths of the night.

Izzy reached through the hole and shaped her hand around the bodywork of the nearest buggy. You could see she was touching something from the way her fingers splayed, but it looked as if she were holding a chunk of outer space.

"Nano black," whispered Izzy. "The blackest black you can get. Completely invisible Stealth Buggies, for night-time travel."

"So cool," breathed Reggie in the background.

Izzy pulled her hand back through the hole and pressed on. At the end of the alleyway was an old door with a familiar sensor next to it. From a plastic bag she pulled out Dad's jelly hand and slapped it on the sensor. A click and the door popped open.

Speaking quietly, Izzy introduced us. "So then everyone. Here's what you've been missing."

Inside was a vast, softly lit room with row upon row of desks. And on each desk was a glowing laptop. Two hundred children gasped, 20 teachers chuckled, one caretaker guffawed and a man in a green suit groaned. Mrs Maynard gave him another cuddle.

Izzy panned slowly around the room, and started to walk around. Unused computers displayed a screensaver of a slowly revolving FF logo, but thirty or forty grown-ups could be seen tapping or scrolling away, mostly on Facebook. None of them looked up. An office with a smoked glass wall faced out onto the room, with shadowy figures moving about behind. Against one wall was a row of vending machines racked up with chocolate, bottles of fizzy drink and crisps. And against another was a row of mobile phones on cords; one parent had his back to us, chatting away. And still nobody noticed Izzy.

She reached the far wall without incident, and a set of double doors signposted *The Vault*.

Just then, everyone in the school hall heard a thudding, thumping sound over the hall speakers. "What's that?"

Izzy whispered.

"Dunno," I said. "Reggie?"

"Sounds like I've got company downstairs," he said. "Hold on, let me check the defences. Back with you soon, Izzy."

It took me a moment to recognise Enid's back garden, now up on the screen. From the camera's elevated viewpoint – Reggie had dangled it on a loop of tape from an upstairs window – a very odd sight flickered into view. Mr Wharton was thumping on the back door and shouting while trying his best to avoid the flailing feet of a body wedged half-way into the catflap. Those school trousers, the dinner stains... it could only be Charlie.

"Open the damn door!" said Mr Wharton.

"Don't do that," came a matter-of-fact voice from inside. "You'll break my neck."

Reggie switched to an inside camera that he had taped to the banisters, looking across the living room and through to the back door. And there was the top half of Charlie, sticking into the room through the catflap. For a boy who might be wearing a back door for the rest of his life, he looked remarkably chirpy. The reason for that was right under his nose: a big bag of sweets, from which he was helping himself at regular intervals.

The door sprung open a couple of inches. But because of the way it hinged it pushed Charlie's head against a kitchen unit, and would move no further. "Ow!" he said, before chewing the finger off someone's massive jelly hands. I didn't even know how he'd got those, or whose they were. Reception children pointed and made "ooh" and "aah" noises.

"Aaargh!" A two-tone cry of frustration could be heard from the other side of the door.

"You OK there, Charlie?" said Reggie.

"Yep, all good here!" he said, looking up at the camera. "Take as long as you like, I'm only half way through this bag. I'll save you some."

"Great work," said Reggie. "We'll leave you to it."

"Rightio!" said Charlie.

"Everything's fine," Reggie said. "Sorry about the interruption. Back to you, Izzy."

"Thanks Reggie," said Izzy, now back on our screen and standing in front of the doors to The Vault. "So you've probably wondered where all those tellies, tablets and phones went when they disappeared." She was really getting the hang of it now, I thought. "The answer is in here."

She slapped Dad's jelly hand on the sensor next to the vault doors. "Access denied. Agents only," intoned the voice. My stomach lurched.

She tried again, without luck.

"I can't get in!" whispered Izzy frantically, still crouched outside the vault. "It's the only hand I've got! And... I think I've been rumbled!"

She pointed the camera across the room; in the opposite corner a huddle of grown-ups were pointing at her, and talking. They nodded, fanned out and slowly advanced towards Izzy.

Behind them a door in the smoked glass opened

inwards. A figure watched from the door, silhouetted against the glowing green light inside. For a moment it paused and bounced on its toes, as if judging the distance.

And then the figure took a handful of easy strides across the room, quickly yet stealthily, sprinting towards Izzy. It was Melissa.

"Thora! Help!" Izzy sounded desperate, and scrabbled at the sensor. I could hear Reggie tapping away in desperation at his computer, but it seemed he was out of ideas too.

The parents were half way across the room now, barely 20 paces away, marching in step with stern expressions. Melissa made easy ground and pushed her way through their cordon. She was seconds away.

Unbidden, a thought came to me. A low-tech snapshot of a message scribbled on a piece of paper. "Izzy! Try password1234!"

"What do you mean?" said Izzy. She was barely listening.

"Try password 1234! On the sensor!"

"How? There's nowhere to type it! Quick, Thora, they've nearly got me!" Izzy spun around: Melissa was looming large, backed by her grim parent stormtroopers.

"Just say it! Say it!"

"Come on Izzy, say it! Say it!" Children's voices from the hall rang out, urging her on.

"Password1234!" shrieked Izzy. "Password1234! Password1234!"

She didn't need to repeat herself – on the first attempt, the door clicked open. "Override activated."

Still chanting the password, Izzy pushed through and

slammed the door shut behind her, sliding down to sit on the floor.

Behind her, thuds and shouts rained down on the door. Izzy sprang away, and cowered, waiting for the inevitable moment when the door would open and The Plan would come to a crashing end.

Chapter 35
THE SWITCH

BUT SECONDS LATER the thumps and shouts stopped – yet the door stayed closed. Silence. We watched as Izzy got slowly and tearfully to her feet.

Casting fearful glances at the door, she faced the camera. "So, yes, I'm sorry about that boys and girls. It seems that not everyone is happy about you knowing what's going on. That's why you need to take a look around."

She flipped the camera and once more the hall was filled with the sound of amazed children. The walls were lined with silver lockers, each with a black address label. Along the top row, numbers 1-47 Bilberry Avenue. Next down: 1-63 Cragside. Then Dale Road. And so on, filling the room.

Izzy reached out and pulled at the door of the nearest locker: 26 The Green. It opened to reveal a treasure trove of electricals: a flatscreen TV, tablets and mobile phones stacked in a basket, a laptop, console and more tucked out of sight.

I took a deep breath. "OK, Reggie. Time to end it. Give me the Prime Minister."

Reggie flicked the main screen back to the PM. He had his horrible calloused feet back up on the table, and was sitting back in his chair with his hands behind his head, sweaty patches on full view. He whistled, long and low. "By heavens," he said softly. "You've really done it now." He reached down for a scratch. "So what happens now, eh? Come along, I haven't got all day."

"Well... " I paused. Maybe 'making it up as you go along' isn't such a rock-solid idea after all. "Reggie? Any ideas?"

"Not too sure," came Reggie's voice over the speakers. "Not got an index card for that."

"Izzy?"

"Dunno," she whispered. "Maybe the grown-ups could put it all back?"

"Put it all back?" snorted the PM, before throwing his head back with a horrible, phlegmy laugh. "Oh yes, that sounds fine, we'll put it all back."

"Hey! Aren't you forgetting something?" I said, annoyed that he somehow seemed to be in control.

"Absolutely not," said the PM. "You hold the cards. If that footage of me gets out, I'll lose the next election for sure. But if you don't know what you want, I suggest we forget all this ever happened, yes?"

I looked around, desperately, as if I could find an idea out there in the hall. Frosty was getting back to his feet, and brushing himself down. Even Kristi had perked up a bit.

There was a moment of silence. Outside the church clock struck half past ten. In the corner of the screen, the word "LIVE" started flashing.

"Give us our fun back!" came a tiny voice. The tiniest of voices, a voice of a mouse. I scanned the room. In the front row, almost invisible behind her classmates, a dinky little girl with curly blonde hair was looking directly at me with piercing blue eyes. I knew her: it was Trinity Hall, the youngest and very much the smallest girl in the school.

"Tell him to give us our fun back!"

"You're right," I said slowly. "That's what you can do. Give us our fun back, Prime Minister."

"What? What on earth do you mean?" The PM looked irritated. "That's exactly what you've got – a village full of fun. Bikes, the country's best play park with lots of time to play in it, no distractions, healthy chores... it's better than my childhood, and that made me the man I am today. You couldn't ask for more than that. What else could you possibly want, you ungrateful squirts?"

"We. Want. Our. Fun. Back," I said firmly. "TV, internet, games, all that stuff."

"Dishwashers!" shouted someone from the back.

"Give us our computer room back!"

"I want my duvet!" yelled someone else.

"Pizzas! Get Pizza Presto to deliver again!"

I barely had to raise a hand for the hall to fall silent. "I know. How about we make a deal?"

"A deal? What kind of deal?" spluttered the PM.

"Our parents keep the money, all of the money. We keep the bikes, and the play park, and get our gadgets back. But you get rid of everything else. The buggies, the cameras, the spies..." I looked across at Kristi, who wouldn't meet my eye.

"I suppose that might be the least worst option," muttered the PM. "Get me out of this fix, at least." He shifted uncomfortably in his chair: perhaps his Superman pants were stuck again.

A big cheer went up from the hall; children punched the air and whooped. "Deal! Deal! Deal!"

I breathed a big sigh of relief. It looked like the nightmare was nearly over.

But through the celebrations I could hear someone shouting. "Help! Help! I'm in trouble! Reggie!"

The picture switched back to Enid's room. And now, instead of pushing at the door, Mr Wharton had grabbed Charlie's feet and was now shoving those instead.

From inside we could see Charlie grabbing onto the surround of the catflap with both hands, trying with all his might not to get pushed into the room. "I can't hold on too much longer, Reggie!"

"Oh dear," said the PM, suddenly smug again. "Looks like your cork is coming unstuck. And then my man Wharton can shut you down, we bring this nonsense to a halt, delete your unfortunate footage and then the show goes on! The deal's orf."

"Thora, look!"

Reggie didn't need telling. We were back with Izzy. She'd turned the camera on the other wall of the vault. It was made of glass, and behind it were shadows of a thousand wires, cables and boxes. The only interruption to the smooth, floor-to-ceiling wall was a huge chrome lever. This thing was enormous, like the shiny clapper of a bell. It was raised to the "off" position, above a sign that said VILLAGE INTERNET: MASTER SWITCH.

"Pull the switch Izzy! Pull it!"

She didn't need telling twice. Izzy reached up above her head, and yanked on the balled end of the lever. It didn't move. She pulled harder, then put the camera on the floor and used both hands. Nothing: she was now hanging from the lever, her legs waggling.

"I can't!" she yelled. "I'm not strong enough!"

In the hall, the comeback king Mr Frost had finally got his nerve back. He straightened his tie, pulled down his green jacket, and walked towards me with a nasty grin on his face.

From the speakers, the PM could be heard. "Give it up, you snivelling little rugrats," he said. "This time the fun's really over."

"I wouldn't be so sure," said a smooth, calm voice.

Izzy screamed.

What happened next was so quick you'd think it had been part of The Plan. But it wasn't, it was life. You make a plan, and try to think of everything. Sometimes you do, usually you don't. But when you don't, occasionally things Just Work Out. Maybe it's luck, maybe it's a reward for all your hard work.

But as I cowered on the stage and prepared for another tussle with The Big Green-Suited Lizard, on the screen we saw a manicured hand reach out and cover Izzy's.

"I think we've all seen enough of The Fun Factor. Maybe it's time someone was on *your* side. Let me help you with that."

Melissa's lycra-clad figure filled our view and with a mighty heave she yanked the lever downwards. Instantly, the equipment behind the glass sprang into life: white lights raced along cables, thousands of blue, red and green LEDs flickered, and a million beeps and chirps rang out like an electronic menagerie.

The children's cheers were interrupted by the sound of material tearing. Back at Enid's house, Mr Wharton had finally won the battle with Charlie's trousers. With a massive *rrrrrip!* Charlie tumbled into the room. Grinning triumphantly, Mr Wharton gave the door a heave and squeezed inside, stepping over Charlie's groaning body.

But Charlie wasn't done yet. Quicker than you'd think for a boy stuffed with sweets and without his trousers, he scrambled to his feet. At the same time there was a clatter as Reggie abandoned his station and sprinted for the stairs. They met on the bottom step. And to my astonishment they slammed the door closed, trapping themselves in the lounge with Mr Wharton.

Reggie turned to Charlie and for a second they looked at each other: Reggie nodded.

"Prepare to die!" shouted Charlie to Mr Wharton, like he'd been practising for it all his life.

That's not actually correct: in fact what he actually shouted was "Prepare to dye!", but it sounded the same of course. And as Charlie yelled, Reggie yanked aside the picture frame and slapped his hand on the sensor three times: Bam! Bam! Bam!

After the first one we heard the familiar words: "This premises is protec – " But she didn't get the chance to remind us about the Dye Protection Technology before

Reggie had slapped the sensor again, and again.

The reaction was instantaneous: a huge explosion made everyone jump, and the screen went blue. But this wasn't an electronic blue, more like a poster paint blue. Gradually, streaks appeared and the blue slid down to the bottom of the screen to reveal an entirely blue room: blue walls, blue furniture, blue carpet and blue people. Reggie, Charlie and Mr Wharton were transformed. Reggie and Charlie walked like zombies around the room, shaking blue liquid from their hands and hair, while Mr Wharton stood still, eyes blinking in astonishment out of his long blue face. An electric blue Shannon appeared at the door to the stairs.

Then there was a fizzing noise, an electronic unhappiness. The image of the blue room flickered and died. The picture cycled crazily through village scenes before ending back in The Vault. Melissa sat on the floor holding a shaking Izzy, who had buried her head in Melissa's shoulder. The screen went black.

Game over.

Epilogue
RIGHT HERE, RIGHT NOW

A RAY OF sunlight wakes me up: I'm not sure what time it is, but probably quite late – maybe 8 o'clock? But it's Saturday: no school today.

"Shutters up," I murmur. With a gentle whirr, hidden motors slowly reveal the outside world. I'm right: the sun is high up above the ridge line, burning off the mist in the valley below.

I yawn and head for the stairs. I put my head around Reggie's door but he must be up already. His curtains are drawn but his duvet is halfway across the floor. Mum will be cross – his new uniform is still scattered across the floor from yesterday. It took them six months to find another headteacher after Frosty took up that offer to appear on *Desert Island Dance Off* and never came back. But the new headteacher is in spring clean mode: new uniform, new staff, new name: it's all change down at Oakdale Village School.

Not that I care too much, now that I'm at the High School. Most mornings Shannon gives me a lift; she's on her way to work anyway, and the factory office doesn't open until 9 o'clock. We sing along to the radio, Shannon and I; Izzy sometimes hitches a ride, but she doesn't know the words like we do. Some mornings a flash of colour will catch my eye and I'll spot Dad across the field on the bridlepath, on his way to work, switching through the trees and bunny hopping over the tree stumps on his Village Bike.

Our balcony is bathed in sunshine. Dad designed it with near-invisible glass panels around the outside. It's as if we're about to ride a magic carpet out over the village and up with the kestrels. That's not a HOUSE 2.0 feature. But then this isn't HOUSE 2.0, it's HOUSE 3.0 – we skipped a version. It turns out that if you want to build a dream house up in the fells, a big dollop of cash from the government is quite helpful. It doesn't harm when your Dad's girlfriend decides she's had enough of the South, sells her house and moves in, too.

"Morning, love," she says, looking up. Melissa is sitting on the balcony in the sun, eating a bowl of fruit and yoghurt, reading the news on her tablet.

"Hi, Mum." I lean down and give her a kiss. (I decided a little while back that if you walk like a mum, talk like a mum, and act like a mum, well then as far as I'm concerned, you are a mum.) "Where's Dad?"

"Not sure, honey. I think he might be with Reggie."

She's right: from upstairs I can hear the sound of gunfire, and cheers: Reggie and Dad are battling to save the city (again). I've told them to turn off the surround sound in the morning, but they take no notice.

"Morning, you guys," croaks Shannon, wandering outside in her nightie. She stretches.

"Hey! I thought you were staying over with your friend?" says Melissa.

"Nah, I wanted to come home. Wouldn't want to miss a Saturday breakfast," says Shannon with a grin. In the middle of the glass-topped table a plate is stacked high with pancakes; she slides a couple onto her own plate before adding a dollop of yoghurt and topping with glistening strawberry halves and slices of mango.

'Maple syrup?' Shannon asks me.

'Just a squirt, please. Not too much.'

Shannon pours a glass of orange juice from the jug, reaches over and pours me one too.

I do the same before heading indoors to the lounge. The sun is bright, so I set the room to Viewing Mode; the windows darken to block out the glare on the opposite wall.

I cycle through the 128 TV channels: there's usually something decent on a Saturday. The picture fills the wall opposite, crystal clear and larger than life. Game shows, a nature programme, an adventure show, the news... I pause. Our Prime Minister is making a statement about something or other, another chapter in what he calls 'A New Era of Humility'.

As far as I can make out, no-one is sure if this particular leopard has changed his spots since that chaotic morning. From the moment the cameras switched to LIVE at half past ten that morning his job appeared to be on the line. Streamed onto the nation's TV screens, a fascinated nation watched as he tried to cheat the children of a small village many hundreds of miles away, doing everything he could to keep his precious experiment from being derailed. But he kept his job, as politicians do, although he certainly isn't the arrogant man he was a year ago.

In the corner of the room our network stack blinks steadily, the computer brains of our new house. Each layer is labelled according to the stuff it controls: Climate, Entertainment, Appliances and Utilities. At the bottom an archive layer gathers dust: "The PM's Pants: Do Not Delete." That bit never got shown, in the end: the public had found out what kind of man he really was without needing to see his Superman underwear. Lucky them. The footage probably isn't even needed these days, but as Reggie says, it's good to have insurance.

There's nothing on TV worth watching. I switch the remote back to Living mode. The sun shines again, I grab my bowl and wander back to the balcony.

"Back so soon?" says Melissa, not looking up.

"Yeah," I say. I look up at the fells, dazzling green against a pure blue sky. "Hey, Mum?"

Melissa puts her tablet to one side and looks at me. "I think I know what's coming," she smiles.

"Maybe," I grin. "Shall we go out for a run?"

THE END

A note from the author

Hi – I'm Mat, the author of The Fun Factor.

Did you enjoy it? What was your favourite bit? Which character did you like the most – was it chess-playing Izzy? Shy Thora? Or perhaps daft Reggie?

Whatever you thought, would you write a review for me? It will be read by loads of other children and parents. You'll be helping them to decide if The Fun Factor is right for them.

It's really easy to do: ask your parent to help you leave a review.

And if you have any questions, comments or things to tell me about The Fun Factor, then go ahead – I'd love to hear from you! You can find ways to contact me on the next few pages.

Finally, I've enjoyed writing The Fun Factor so much that I'm working on another book I think you'll like. If you want to hear more about it, ask your parent to sign up for my emails at matwaugh.co.uk.

Mat

About me

I'M A FATHER of three young girls. I'm often tired. These two things are connected.

I live in Tunbridge Wells, which is a lively, lovely town in the south east of England.

Small boys scare me – they do too much running, and not enough drawing. But I'm petrified by the thought of three teenage girls.

When I was seven I wrote to Clive King. He's the author of my favourite childhood book, *Stig of the Dump*, which is about a caveman who lives in a house made out of rubbish. I asked Clive if there was going to be a sequel, but he said no.

I've had lots of writing and editing jobs, but mostly for other people.

I forgot: I also had a crazy year when I thought I wanted to be a teacher. But then I found out how hard teachers work, and that you have to buy your own biscuits. So I stopped, and now I just visit schools to eat theirs.

I always wanted to write my own stories, but I could never find the right moment. So I waited until I had children and had no spare time at all.

I love hearing from readers. Funny stuff, silly stuff, serious stuff. If that's you, then you can email me or contact me at matwaugh.co.uk – just ask your parents first.

Also by Mat Waugh

Cheeky Charlie (Book 1)
Cheeky Charlie: Bugs and Bananas (Book 2)
Cheeky Charlie: King of Chaos (Book 3)
Cheeky Charlie: He Didn't Mean It (Book 4)

He's three, she's eight. Together they're trouble.

A new series of family adventures starring the biggest little chaos-magnet around. Oh, and Charlie's big sister, Harriet, who's definitely done nothing wrong. Nothing at all, so why are you even asking?

Expect daft dads, rude grown-ups who get what they deserve and a polite sprinkling of bottom jokes.

Want a taster? Grab a free book at Mat's website.

Printed in Great Britain
by Amazon

32809792R00147